PRIVATE PROPERTY

SKYE WARREN

CHAPTER ONE

A GUST OF wind rocks the Toyota Prius.

I clench my teeth together. I'm pretty sure this compact eco-friendly car wasn't designed to travel up a mountain. Rain falls in sheets, heavy on the thin roof. Through the window a half moon reveals an endless climb. I cling to the plastic handle, shivering against the worn fabric of the seat.

They didn't have mountains this high in Houston. I thought the plane ride was scary, but this hour and a half drive is worse. Much worse. I knew Eben Cape was on the coast, but I pictured something sandy with gentle waves.

Not steep cliffs that drop into nothing.

"Do you come this way often?" I ask.

"Nope."

Not a talkative one, my driver. He had a low rating on the app, but that's what you get for an economy ride share. The pounding of rain unnerves me. As does the slope on the road.

Water will make it slippery. I'd almost ask him to turn around, except that seems more dangerous on this narrow road. The only way left is forward. And up.

My ears do that strange hollow feeling I got when the airplane took off. I can't see much in the dark, can't hear anything. It's a surreal sensation, like floating through space.

I look down at my phone. Its light almost blinds me.

No signal.

If I lost signal, then maybe the driver did, too. "Do you still see the map?"

"Only one place this leads," he says, almost shouting to be heard over the storm. "The Coach House. Nothing to do but keep going now."

The Coach House. That sounds comforting. A lot better than the number and street address I punched into the app. I'm picturing something with sturdy bricks and a birdbath. I close my eyes and hold the image in my mind, clutching my phone so tight it hurts.

I know precious little about the family I'm going to work for. Only that a man recently got custody of his niece. I wonder if he's a fisherman. Maybe he catches lobsters out in that wild ocean spray. He'd wear rubber boots and have a white beard.

The car jerks suddenly, pulling out of its end-less turn, the whole frame rocking on the tires as we reach some pinnacle. I let out a squeak that's swallowed by the gales of wind.

Shadows shift through the windshield. Some-thing looms ahead of us—large like another mountain to climb. Except it's not a mountain. It's a house. No, more than that. It's a mansion. *Don't stop,* I think. *Don't stop here.* There's something forbidden about this place. I'm too practical to believe in ghosts, but this place feels somehow haunted.

The car skids to a stop, the brakes pumping in some automated fashion to stop the slide. The man already has his blinker on, ready to turn around in the small space as soon as I'm out the door. I peer through my window at the mass of slick night-blackened stone.

"Listen," I say, my hands shaking as I pull up my phone. It still has no signal. The map of Maine has no little dot to show where I am. It only spins and spins. "Are you sure this is the right place? I don't see a street number written anywhere."

"This is the Coach House," he says, impatient now. He still doesn't turn. I'm talking to the back of his head. To the side of his shoulder.

"Okay. Okay." He doesn't want to talk to me anymore, and maybe that doesn't matter. It's not really for him. I'm pumping myself up. For someone who never set foot outside Harris County her whole life, this trip has been like shaking up a goldfish in a bag. "I can do this."

No answer to that.

"I'm going to walk in that house. And work there. And live there. For a year."

He turns the radio on. The Weeknd vibrates through the tinny speakers. It's not precisely reassuring, the way the music fights with the storm for dominance and loses. I open the door. Wind tries to keep it closed, but I use my body weight to half-step, half-fall onto the soggy grass. I drag the carry-on luggage I picked up from Walmart last week with me.

The car inches forward, the door hanging open, rain pooling on the dark fabric, and I jump forward to slam the door so he doesn't end up driving down the mountain that way.

Tires slide against wet ground. Mud flings against me in a hard splatter.

Great.

I head to the front door, which naturally does not have much of an overhang. Rain slicks my clothes to my body as I ring the electronic doorbell, trying to school my expression to one of calmness in case anyone's watching with their phone. A *bong* reverberates from inside, but no one answers the door. I count to twenty in my head. Then thirty. Then sixty.

I ring again. Nothing.

The cold and wet has numbed me almost to my core, but worry begins to seep in. What if there's no one here? What if I'm at the wrong house? What if the entire upscale nanny agency was a setup, and I'm being filmed on some kind of terrible Netflix mockumentary about how desperate poor people are to find a job?

No. *Listen,* I tell myself. *They probably can't hear the doorbell over the storm.*

This time I knock, but the heavy wood seems to stifle the vibration. It might as well be made from the same stone as the rest of the house for all the sound it makes.

I try to shield my phone from the rain with my body. I don't have the latest fancy waterproof Apple device. Mine is the free-with-twelve-month-contract phone. With no signal. *Don't panic, Janey girl.* That's what Dad used to call me. I can still hear it sometimes, even if the voice is probably made up and sounds nothing like him.

If I'm in the wrong place, with no lights for miles around me, high in a mountain, and no phone signal, I would sit down in the sludge and cry.

Therefore, that can't be happening.

I have to believe that the Rochester family of two is inside this house.

It's only a matter of getting to them.

Four floors rise above the tallest point of the mountain. There isn't a strong light to let me know that someone's home, but that doesn't mean it's empty anyway. The house has a sort of melancholy presence that makes me feel like someone's inside.

I head for the side of the mansion, dragging my suitcase behind me. If no one's answering the front door, there's probably someone in the back.

As soon as I round the corner, I realize exactly how massive the structure is. It stretches along the cliffs in rows of dark windows across a pale stone face. The farther away I get from the gravel road, the more rocky the terrain becomes. I squint down at my feet, trying to make sure I stand on grass or rock. The mud itself is too slippery.

That's what I'm doing when I hear the roar of an engine.

I jump back as white lights blind me, moving

in wild arcs across my body, across the building. It's a car. *It's a car!* And it's coming for me. I scream and back up against the wall as if it can somehow protect me from the careening vehicle.

Lights flash and flicker. The stone is freezing cold through my clothes.

And then stillness.

As suddenly as the headlights appeared, they stop moving.

I'm still pinned against the mansion like a butterfly in a frame, but at least I'm still alive. A car door slams, and then there's a large shadow looming over me.

"What the fuck are you doing? You could have been killed," says the shadow.

Somehow his voice booms over the rain, as if it's above ordinary things like the weather. I open my mouth to reply, but pinned butterflies can't speak. Everyone knows this. Shock holds my throat tight even as my heart pounds out of my chest.

"You don't belong here. This is private property."

I swallow hard. "I'm Jane Mendoza. The new nanny. Today is my first day."

There's silence from the shadow. In the stretching silence he turns into a man. A large one who seems impervious to the cold. "Jane," he says, testing my name. "Mendoza."

He says it with this northeastern accent I recognize from the Uber driver. Mend-ohhh-sah. In Texas, most people were used to Mexican last names. I'm wondering if that will be different in Maine. Maybe I would do a better job of defending myself if I weren't about to get hypothermia, if I hadn't just traveled two thousand miles for the first time in my life.

All I can hear are the words *you don't belong here.*

I've never belonged anywhere, but definitely not on this cliffside. "I work here. I'm telling the truth. You can ask inside. If we can get inside, I'm sure Mr. Rochester will tell you."

"He will."

I can't tell if it's disbelief in his tone. "Yes, he knows I'm coming. The Bassett Agency sent me. They told him I'm coming. He's probably waiting inside for me right now."

"No," he says. "I'm not."

My stomach sinks. "You're Mr. Rochester."

"Beau Rochester." He sounds grim. "I didn't get an email, but I haven't checked lately. I've been busy with… other things."

I fumble with my phone, which is incurably

wet at this point. "I can show you. They sent my resume. And then the contract? Well, that's what they told me anyway—"

He's not listening. He turns around and circles back to the driver's side of the vehicle, which I can see now isn't a car, but is instead some kind of rough-terrain four-wheel thing. There are apparently no windows, only metal bars forming a crude frame. The kind of thing a rancher might use to move around his property or a good old boy might use for recreation.

I have no idea why this particular man has one, or is out using it tonight, until he turns off the lights. The engine goes quiet. He returns to me holding something small and shivering beneath his jacket. He shoves it into my freezing hands, and I fumble with my phone before pushing it into my jeans pocket.

"Here," he says. "You're good at taking care of things, right?"

There's a spark of fur covering tiny bones. It takes me a second of curling it close to my body to realize that it's a kitten. It mews, more movement than sound, its small mouth opening to show small white teeth. "Why do you have your kitten outside in the storm?"

"It's not mine. I saw it walking along the cliffs

from my window when it started raining. Then it slipped and fell over the side. It took me this long to go down and search for him."

Shock roots me to the ground. "The kitten fell off a cliff?"

"Consider this your interview. You keep the small animal alive. You get the job."

I cuddle the poor kitten close, though I'm sure my body provides precious little heat. He and I are both soaked through. "He just fell off a cliff. He needs a vet, not a bedtime story."

The man. Beau. No, I can't call him by his first name. Mr. Rochester. He makes a sweeping motion with his hand toward the vehicle. "You can take the ATV anywhere on the cape. I seriously doubt you're going to find a vet open right now."

He doesn't wait to see what my answer will be. He stalks toward the house. My suitcase lolls in a particularly large puddle. Probably everything is soaked inside. He picks it up like it weighs nothing and carries it with him. I'm left following behind, as bedraggled and lost as the kitten I'm holding. It sinks its claws into me, apparently deciding I'm the safest bet in the storm.

Mr. Rochester presses numbers on a keypad, and the door swings open.

CHAPTER TWO

APPARENTLY HE WAS serious about this being an interview.

He leans back against the granite counter and folds his arms, watching me with a critical eye. Everything in here gleams in a hardwood and dark metal kind of way. It makes my scruffy, muddy appearance even more obvious as it's reflected back off a hundred surfaces. Mr. Rochester himself looks coldly handsome. It isn't right for a man so hard to look almost beautiful. The kitchen lights reveal piercing brown eyes and thick brows. His nose is long and flat on the top. His mouth is pressed into a thin line of displeasure.

I hold the drenched kitten away from me, trying to see if anything is broken. Not that I would know what to do about it if it were. It wriggles in what seems to be a normal kitten fashion? I have very little experience with pets. My life is divided into two halves. The before and after. Before, my dad was allergic to pets but he always promised that when I got older I could get a puppy. After he died, I bounced through foster homes. Occasionally there'd be a dog. Or two. Or three. In the last house there was an entire pack of them who roamed the house and the woods nearby as if they were the same thing. They weren't exactly domesticated.

Mr. Rochester lifts an eyebrow, clearly unimpressed with my nanny abilities.

"I've never had a cat," I say, though it comes out more like a question.

"Then act like it's a baby." His dark hair will turn brown when it dries. It's a stark contrast to my black curls, which stay the same color wet. Now that we're inside I can see that he's tall, built, and white. A green sweater hugs a broad chest and narrow waist. Wet denim cling to muscled thighs and drips onto the marble tile.

"You know, I already signed a yearlong contract with the agency for this position. We had multiple rounds of interviews, including one that was videotaped for you."

He shrugs, unimpressed with this. "You're locked in for a year. I'm not. I can fire you anytime I want if you don't do a good enough job."

Great. Holding the kitten in one arm like a football, I search through the drawers and cabinets for something marked *Emergency Pack for Stray Kittens.*

All I end up with is a large metal mixing bowl and a stack of flour sack dish towels.

I take him to a white ceramic sink and fill the bowl with warm water. Without any actual training in animal care, I'm working under the knowledge that a hot bath sounds amazing to me right now. It's the only thing I can think of that would work this chill from my bones.

When the water's the right temperature I fill the bowl only a few inches and then settle the kitten inside. She responds with a small, broken meow that hurts my heart.

"I know," I murmur to her, my back turned to Mr. Rochester. It feels like me and the kitten are in this thing together. Sure, the guy saved the kitten's life, but he doesn't seem very invested in her survival. He stands there watching me like we're a television show. Like a survival reality show where they throw a girl and a kitten in the ocean to see if they live. "I know you're cold right now. And probably freaked out. This place is scary, but you'll be okay."

"Are you planning to cook him for dinner?"

Mr. Rochester asks amiably.

"Listen." I carefully lift the kitten from the water and dry her off using the dish towels, one by one. I try to move quick so she'll get warm, but I also have to be careful. She feels like he's made of toothpicks. One wrong move, and she'll snap. "There's no *business* underneath, so I think we can assume she's a girl. And you could be helpful by getting some warm milk or whatever it is cats like to eat instead of just criticizing what I'm doing."

As soon as the words are out of my mouth, I wish I could take them back.

I don't have a ton of experience with job interviews. I worked at the diner near my foster home and as a cashier at a grocery store when I moved out, but those weren't really interviews. I filled out an application and got a call back. The nanny agency interviewed me several times, but they seemed okay with my rambling answers about taking care of my foster siblings and babysitting and volunteering at the food bank. Despite my relative inexperience with interviews, I feel like talking back and asking him to get a bowl of milk is probably not the best thing to say.

But when I turn around, he's already reaching inside the wide stainless steel fridge. Even in this quick glimpse I can see that it's mostly empty. He does find a carton of milk, half full. In a few moments he's found a saucer that he pours into.

"Thanks," I murmur, accepting the saucer from him. I wrap the kitten like a burrito using the last dry dish towel and then set her down in front of the milk.

She shoves her face into the liquid, making her nose white.

I can't help it. It makes me laugh, but then I catch Mr. Rochester's eye. He has a strange expression. Strange because it's less severe and judgy than the one he'd had a minute before. As soon as he sees me looking at him, he grabs the milk and stows it back in the fridge.

Once the kitten understands the way milk works, she laps it up.

I'm going to have to find some cat food and probably google a million pages about caring for kittens, but I think she's doing okay. I have to hope that if a bone were broken, I'd be able to tell. Maybe it's true what they say about cats having nine lives.

She probably used up a couple of them falling off that massive cliff.

"Sorry," I say without looking up. I'm sitting with one leg under me, the other curled up beneath my chin, watching the kitten. "About saying you should be helpful."

I read the fine print in the contract. Enough to know that the penalty for breaking it early would be severe… for me. I only get paid the bulk of it after the year is over. And I don't get that if I leave before then. Of course the strictness only works one way. He can fire me anytime. I just didn't think he'd consider doing it on the first night.

"Don't worry about it."

"I just wasn't expecting the whole kitten interview thing."

"You can keep the job. For now."

I let out a huff of exhausted laughter. "Thanks."

"Come on," he says. "I'll show you to your room. You can share with the kitten."

Great. My suitcase has been dripping onto the marble floor this whole time. I grab the warm bundle of fur and the suitcase and follow him down the hallway. We pass a series of rooms with sofas and dining tables and pianos and then more sofas. The place is massive. It's more like a hotel lobby where hundreds of people could pass through, instead of a house for two people.

Everything looks expensive and even comfortable, but it doesn't feel like a home.

A full wall of windows exposes the storm in all its glory. Maybe some people like watching nature use the earth like a drum, but after being out in it I'm still shivering. There's a trail of muddy water behind me that I'll probably have to clean up tomorrow. Right now I'm just desperate for a chance to get into some dry clothes.

He turns a corner and we head down a long hallway with a series of closed doors. Like the windows outside, they're dark and nondescript and innately full of secrets.

A small gesture. His voice is low in the dark hallway. "That's her bedroom. Paige. The reason for your position. You'll meet her tomorrow."

The reason for your position. There's no warmth in his voice, even though he's talking about a six-year-old little girl. "You're her uncle?"

"Correct," he says, his voice matter of fact. And cold. Colder than outside.

I'm almost running to keep up. So I slam into him when he stops suddenly. One minute I'm striding along a corridor, and the next I'm plastered against him, cold clothes against cold clothes, warm body against warm body, my face pressed into his back.

"I'm so sorry," I say, heat climbing my neck as I step back.

He opens one of the doors, and only now do I realize I should have been counting. Every single door looks the same. The distance between them is the same. There's no artwork or rugs in this hallway. Barren. That's how it looks. How it feels. The room is no different. There's a bed in the middle. A nightstand. An open door revealing a small bathroom. A closed door that I assume leads to a closet. There's not even a rug or lamp to make the room feel lived in.

"This is yours," he says. "Your space when you aren't working."

"Me and the cat."

His lips quirk. "Right. You and the cat."

I have to squeeze by him to get into the room. We only touched for a second, but it was electric. I can still feel the currents running through me. Even getting close to him feels like heat. I wheel my soggy luggage into a corner and then settle the kitten in the middle of the bed. I flick on the light in the bathroom and blink against the glare. I'm pretty sure we need a litter box or something like that, but I'm too freezing and tired to worry about it now.

I turn to face Mr. Rochester. Beau Rochester.

"Well," I say, tangling my hands together. "Thanks so much for showing me to my room.

And for the... you know, the welcome. And everything. I want you to know that I'm so grateful for the opportunity to be here, and I'm going to work so hard to make sure that—"

"You're freezing," he says, almost gently.

I'm freezing. And I'm rambling. "Right. I'm cold. You're cold. The kitten is cold, but more importantly, Paige and I are going to get along great. I'm so excited to get started."

I'm not sure why, but in that moment, I look down. And I see that my nipples are hard points against the fabric of my bra and the T-shirt I wore on the plane. I fold my arms in front of me, the movement protective and wildly obvious. If he didn't know my nipples were standing at attention before, then he definitely knows now.

Reluctantly I meet his dark gaze. Oh, he knew. He definitely knew.

"Your job isn't to be best friends with Paige," he says.

"Right," I say, even though I don't know where he's going with this.

"Your job with her is the same as it is with the kitten. Keep her alive and keep her out of my hair. That's what you're getting paid to do. Understand?"

In both the before and after of my life, I believed in the value of family. I always knew my father loved me. And cared for me. And when he was gone, when I was cold and lonely and afraid, I knew it was because I no longer had a family. "But she's your niece."

"I'm not a parent. I'm a businessman. And in the business world, she's what we call a liability. Something I'm required to pay. An expense. A loan. The wrong side of the balance sheet."

My breath sucks in. "She's a child."

His gaze flicks down to where my arms cover my breasts. "So were you, not that long ago."

For the first time I'm aware of him as more than a shadow shouting in the rain, as more than my new employer. I become aware of him as a man. And he's aware of me as a woman. There's a form of power in that mutual understanding.

There are years between us. How old is he? Some number greater than thirty, for sure. The hard planes of his face are strong, mature. His eyes are world weary. I would almost expect there to be gray in his hair for how jaded he appears, but instead there's a lush black.

Too many years for a potential relationship, even if he were interested in rain-soaked nannies and I were interested in cold-blooded men. But the spark runs between us anyway, our bodies giving way to chemistry when our minds should know better.

I need to end this awareness, this mutual interest, the physicality of standing here while both of us are cold and shivering, our clothes clinging to our skin. "Good night," I say, but the word comes out low and smoke-filled, as if I meant it to be tempting.

I've never meant to be tempting in my life.

He does not answer me with words. Instead he closes the door in my face.

CHAPTER THREE

I WAKE UP at six a.m. to an overcast day and texts from Noah. His face appears next to his words, that lazy grin, his dirty blond hair. The kitten stretches beside me and mews, clearly interested in finding more milk for the day.

How was the flight? Did you meet the family?

Shana covered your shift yesterday. Pissed off a bunch of your regulars.

Are you ready to come home yet?

At least my waterlogged cell phone continues to work.

Noah was placed in my last foster home before me. He took me under his wing. Taught me the unspoken rules. Snuck food from the kitchen when I was punished and made to go without dinner. He's my best friend in the world, and I hate disappointing him.

Met the uncle, I swipe into my phone. *Seems kinda strict.*

We know all about strict. The foster home we shared was built on ever-shifting rules that we would inevitably fail. It was cold and uncomfortable and filled with fleas—but it was a roof over our heads and questionable food on a plate each evening.

He texts back right away. *Miss you already.*

Guilt sits heavy in my stomach. He didn't want me to sign this contract, but I couldn't keep working shifts at the diner and the grocery store forever. I barely earned enough to cover my share of the rent, much less what it would take to go to college.

Only three percent of kids who age out of the foster care system ever get a college degree. I'm going to be in that three percent even if it kills me.

I'm going to trade in this one year for a new future.

This job will change my life.

Assuming I keep it. That seems uncertain based on the way Beau Rochester spoke last night.

Leaving the kitten in bed, I shower quickly and step out of the room with my hair still wet. I don't have to count the doors to know which one belongs to the child. Paige. That's her name. Paige Rochester. The door is open, and there's an argument in progress.

"It's twenty degrees outside," says a low voice

I recognize as Beau. "You can't walk around in a T-shirt from Reading Rainbow and a goddamn tutu."

A small but furious voice. "It's Reading *Railroad,* and it costs two hundred dollars."

"I don't care what it costs. If it's not long sleeves and pants and socks and a sweater, it's not going to fucking—I mean, it's not going to fly."

When I reach the doorway, I'm confronted with the view of a man, six foot something, built with lean muscles and a hard expression, facing off with a mutinous little girl wearing a red shirt with a black railway engine on it and a black tutu.

Both man and little girl look extremely stubborn and severe about the issue. It would be almost comical, how alike they look despite their differences, if I didn't worry I was about to be caught in the middle of this dispute.

"Good morning," I say brightly.

Mr. Rochester glances back at me. "Thank God you're here. Surely dressing a child in the morning is part of your job description."

"Yes," I say, drawing the word out. This is heading for a disaster if I'm thrown into her life this way, as some kind of enforcer. Yes, I'll have to impose rules on her but she also needs to see me as a caregiver. As a kind person in her life. "But we haven't been introduced."

He gets a sardonic glint in his eye. "This is Paige Marie Rochester. The reason for your new paycheck. Paige, this is Jane... what was your last name again?"

"Mendoza. Jane Mendoza." I give the girl a tentative smile. "I hope you'll call me Jane."

Her mutinous expression doesn't change.

I take a step into her bedroom, shivering at the chill that pervades the air.

Unlike my room it's bursting with color. It's painted pink with posters of unicorns and dragons pinned up. Her bedspread sports pink-red roses. Despite the profusion of girly pink, it's clear where this girl's true passion lies. A Monopoly board dominates the center of the room, pieces spread across, real estate cards in disarray. Crinkled money peeks out from the bottom of the dresser and from inside drawers.

I sit down on the bed, trying to act casual, as if I attempt to befriend grieving six-year-olds every day. "I'd love to get to know you better, Paige. What kind of things do you like? I already know you like Monopoly. I've played that game, but I'm not very good at it. I bet you are."

She doesn't answer.

Mr. Rochester lists things like he's cataloging

some strange species of animal. "Her favorite hobbies are ignoring the things I ask her to do, throwing things on the ground. And saying that she wishes I was dead. Oh, and she demands Pop-Tarts for dinner."

In that short statement, I see how the last few months have unfolded between them. I knew that her parents had died in a tragic accident, relatively recently. But somehow I assumed that her uncle, like any caring family member, would treat her gently. He'd put up pictures of the people she lost. Since he has money, he'd probably get her therapy, too.

They would be a unit. A sad but loving unit.

That whole image goes up in flames. They've clearly been locked in a battle for a lot longer than this morning. I knew I'd have to work hard at this job, but now it feels dangerously close to impossible. Except I need this to work.

"Well," I say, keeping my voice even. "I suppose the first thing to do is figure out what to wear." Her T-shirt is not much proof against the cold. She's got bare feet beneath a black tulle skirt. I agree with Mr. Rochester in theory. But if I demand long sleeves and pants and socks and a sweater, we're never going to leave this room. I might as well insist she turn lead into gold while

I'm at it. Instead I head over to the dresser where I find a bunch of colorful clothes all jumbled together as if they came in a trash bag and were dumped out. No attempt at folding or organizing has been made. I suppose it's good that they seem clean.

I dig around and find a thin Gucci hoodie. "How about this, as a compromise? You can keep what you're wearing, add this, and then be comfortable around the house?"

"You smell bad," she says to me.

Great.

Mr. Rochester raises his eyebrows. "Ms. Mendoza, can I speak with you a moment?"

I follow him into the hallway.

"Do you have this under control?"

Under control? No. "We'll be fine."

"Right. That's how it seemed in there." His voice is sardonic. Light streams through the doorway, casting his handsome face in sharp lines. His expression looks stern. It's scary, enough to make my stomach turn to knots. And also somehow hot.

Warmth floods my cheeks. "I'll figure it out."

His lip quirks as if he knows what I'm thinking. "She'll walk all over you."

I lift my chin. "You hired me to do a job. Let

me do it."

His dark eyes flash. He likes me strong and defiant. For a moment it looks like he's going to reach for me. Touch me. His hand actually rises. It's inches from my face. Then it drops. "I'll be in my study if you need me." He pauses with a hard look. "Don't need me."

Then he's gone, leaving me alone.

I walk back into the room with a small child who probably hates my guts.

This is not precisely a new situation for me. I helped the younger kids in foster care. That, along with a very nice letter from my social worker testifying to that, allowed me to get this job.

However, I only had to get them dressed and onto the school bus each morning. And get them fed after school and into bed. I didn't have to actually teach them their lessons each day. And they were probably going to move to another home in a few months. It would be rare to stay together an entire year. The bar was a lot lower there, basically.

I examine the hoodie. It looks like it's never been used. "This is the same color as community chest. That's cool, isn't it?"

"Nice try, lady."

I drop the hoodie back into the drawer.

Yeah, it wasn't going to be that easy. *She'll walk all over you.*

"Listen," I say to her. "I know you don't have any reason to trust me right now, but I promise I'm on your side. I'm just here to make your life easier, really."

Nothing.

Time to pull out the big guns. "I have a kitten in my room."

She looks suspicious but interested.

"If you're very gentle, you can pet her. And I'll even let you name her."

I take a page from Mr. Rochester's book and head out of the room without waiting to see if she'll follow. I don't look back, but I do listen very carefully. Sure enough there's the gentle swish of motion that lets me know she's coming, too.

The kitten had seemed like a wet ball of fur and bones last night. Now she's mostly wide eyes and large pointy ears. Her hair is a mixture of black, white, and caramel colors. She stands at the edge of the bed and meows when she sees us.

Paige lets out a sound of delight and drops to her knees by the bed. She immediately falls into baby talk. "Oh who's a good little kitten, it's you, it's you, you're so little and so sweet."

The kitten leans forward and boops its nose against hers.

"Mr. Rochester—that is, Beau—he rescued her from the storm last night," I say, hoping that it will win him some points with the child. He clearly needs them.

She doesn't take her eyes off the kitten. "Maybe she didn't *want* to be rescued. Did he think of that? No, of course not, he does whatever he wants. Like a *man*."

I don't bother telling her that the kitten had fallen off the cliff. That would only give her nightmares, probably. And I don't tell her that the kitten might have frozen to death outside. She doesn't need more thoughts of death in her life.

Besides, she isn't really talking about the kitten right now.

She's talking about herself.

"I'm sure he's only trying to help," I say softly, though in my mind I can still hear him saying, *in the business world, she's what we call a liability. Something I'm required to pay. An expense. A loan. The wrong side of the balance sheet.* "Let's go downstairs, and we can find something for the kitten to eat. What do you think she would like? And we can get breakfast for ourselves."

Paige scrunches her small nose in concentration.

This is a pivotal moment. She wants to refuse anything to do with me, but she also wants to help take care of the kitten. Which one will win out right now? She scoops the tiny thing against her chest and stares straight ahead, all without saying a word.

I take that as a sign that I should lead the way.

Ironic, since I have no idea where the kitchen is.

I head out of the room toward the direction of the stairs. We climb down together, me keeping an eye on both of them since the girl is clearly distracted and halfway in love with the kitten. She keeps making moon eyes at it instead of holding on to the rail. I'm too nervous about our tenuous peace to tell her to be careful, so instead I just use my body to block a potential fall.

We make it down safely and head past the miles of rooms. Living rooms. Sitting rooms. Formal rooms. Parlors? I don't really know the difference between them all. I'm used to one central space with a TV blaring and too many butts to fit on the sofa.

Even *before*, my family had a modest suburban house, not a mansion like this.

The smell of bacon and coffee pulls me in the

right direction. We wind up back in the kitchen where I nursed the kitten back to warmth last night. It doesn't feel quite real, that "interview" with Mr. Rochester, like something that happened in a dream.

An older white woman stands at the stove, flipping something. Pancakes. My stomach growls audibly. I didn't eat anything since before I got on the plane yesterday.

"Breakfast ends at eight," she says without turning around. "I'm the housekeeper. Call me Mrs. Fairfax. Show up on time or be hungry."

"Thank you," I say, flashing a quick smile at Paige so she doesn't feel hurt by the abrupt comments. "We'll definitely come down in time to eat."

"I don't change diapers," she continues. "Or wipe dirty faces. Don't get paid to do that. Only cook and clean up around the place. Sweep the floors. Stock the fridge."

Indignation rises in my throat, but I force it back. I don't mind her being rude to me, but she has no cause to be rude to the child, who clearly is well out of diapers. "Great. Then I'll give you a list of some things to get. Starting with plenty of fruits for snacks for a growing child, vegetables to cook for dinner, and kitten food."

The woman's eyes narrow, but she gives me a brusque nod.

I haven't made a new friend here, but at least we understand each other.

There are platters of pancakes, eggs, bacon, and salmon on the counter. I find two large plates and fill them up, one for me and one for Paige. Then I find a saucer and put tiny bits of eggs, bacon, and salmon on there for the kitten. I set them out on the blue kitchen table.

Paige puts the kitten down in front of her plate and urges her to eat. "There you go, little kitten. Have this fish. Have some really good, salty fish. Yes. It's so good for you."

She uses a "mom" voice for the last part, and my heart breaks, thinking that her mom would have said similar things to her about fish and vegetables. Only six months ago her mother was in this world, caring for her little girl. Now she's gone, and Paige seems adrift.

CHAPTER FOUR

Mr. Rochester never appears for dinner. I heat the food for him and even set a plate when Paige and I sat down to eat, but he never shows up. After dinner I tackle the alarmingly large pile of dirty laundry in Paige's closet, and make it my goal to organize her clothes. "Paige. Where is the washing machine?"

"I dunno."

"Then how do you clean your clothes?"

Wide eyes. "Mommy did that."

It's only been a few months since her mother died. It's a sensitive issue, and I wouldn't normally press, but we do need clean clothes. Especially if they haven't been cleaned in all that time. "Your mommy would walk around with a laundry basket, right? Where did she go with it?"

A stiff shrug.

I'm going to need my clothes cleaned at some point. Only a few pairs of jeans and shirts fit into my carry-on suitcase. More important than that, however, is cleaning Paige's clothes. It's part of my job to take care of her. "Can you help me find it?"

"A washing machine?"

"Mhmm. A big white machine that looks like a fridge only shorter." My apartment back in Houston doesn't have one. I walk three blocks with a garbage bag to the washeteria twice a week. I hope I don't have to trek down this mountain with laundry to make this happen.

She looks reluctant to leave the couch, which I understand. The wind whistles through the cracks on the large windows. Heavy clouds threaten to unleash more rain.

We check the kitchen, checking for some small door leading to a laundry room.

We walk through the dining room and living rooms, where clearly a washer and dryer don't belong.

We reach the back of the house which leads to a garage. There's a car that looks low and sleek, a hint of red paint peeking out from beneath a gray plastic cover. There's also a black SUV that looks like it would have no trouble on the slippery roads up and down the mountain. And there's the four-wheeler with its large grippy wheels and giant headlights, now dark.

This should be pay dirt. It's the perfect place for a washer and dryer. There's lots of room, lots of concrete, and insulation from the house to keep the sound from getting inside. Nope. I cover the whole perimeter but don't find anything.

When I reach the door again, Paige is gone. She was standing right here.

"Paige?"

The shadows seem longer than before. Darker.

I retrace my steps down the hallway. A door is left ajar. Was that closed before? I open and reveal a stairway leading into inky blackness. A basement. Why didn't I think of that? We don't have basements in Houston. Something about being at sea level. But of course we're not at sea level here. In fact we're far above the sea on a cliff.

"*Paige?*"

Did she go back to the kitchen? Did she go to her room? She's padding around the house in her nightgown. There's a distinct chill coming from the basement. I don't want to go down there. It's a feeling. A sense of dread.

Something ephemeral pulls me down the stairs.

Step after step onto creaking wooden stairs.

My bare foot touches the floor. Cold concrete

registers before something bright jumps out at me—a wild animal with blonde hair and a mischievous grin. "Boo!" she says.

My heart thumps in wild disarray. "Oh my God."

"Can I have a Pop-Tart?"

I let out a shuddery breath. "You scared me. And you already ate dinner."

"I'm still hungry."

"Is this where the washer and dryer are? Down here?"

She shrugs and then skips up the steps, presumably to go in search of Pop-Tarts. Frankly, I'm going to need a Pop-Tart after this. That was honestly terrifying. I fumble my hand along the wall, picking up cobwebs as I go, before I find the light switch. They blink on with brightness that makes me squint, revealing a large workroom with benches, saws, and other tools.

And in the corner, an ancient-looking washer and dryer.

I start a load of laundry and pile up the rest around the washing machine like a shrine to cleanliness. It will probably take a few days to get everything clean and folded.

Paige allows herself to be wrangled after eating one and a half strawberry Pop-Tarts. We brush her teeth—again, since she ate. And I put her to bed after reading three books to her.

It was a hard first day of work, but relatively successful I think?

There's only one problem.

It's freezing cold in my room.

Even wearing all the layers of clothes I brought with me, I'm still shivering. They just don't make winter clothes for Houston. We'd only use them two days out of the year anyway. When I was moving around, making food for Paige or cleaning after her, I was warm enough.

It's only when I'm in my room at night that I turn into a block of ice.

I could ask Mr. Rochester for an extra blanket tomorrow.

But I'm freezing cold now.

I'm shivering in the bed, unable to sleep. For hours.

At this rate I'm going to be a zombie tomorrow.

My nightgown is a pale gray shift that does little against the chill. I pad into the hallway. Everything's dark. Quiet. I know better than to wake anyone up.

This is a wealthy house, though. A well-stocked house. There ought to be a linen closet somewhere with an extra blanket. Maybe even a fluffy pair of socks, though that might be wishful thinking.

Though there wasn't one downstairs when I was searching for the washing machine. Nothing that I can remember in the kitchen, the dining room, the living room, the garage, or even the basement.

That leaves this second floor to search.

I open the door next to mine. It reveals a room that's much larger, with a massive bed in the middle. It feels like I walked into the middle of someone's room—not another guest room like mine. There's a man's watch on the nightstand. So maybe this is Mr. Rochester's room? But there's a teacup on the other side of the bed, as if a woman also lives here.

A jacket is slung over an armchair. It's very casual. The way someone would leave their room if they intended to be back soon, but there's a staleness to the air. The blanket on the bed—no one's using that. Shadows from clothes peek out of the closet, but it feels wrong to touch anything here, a little bit like walking on a grave.

I creep back out quietly and close the door.

The next room is clearly someone's study. There's a large wooden desk engraved with scrolls, tall built-in bookshelves, and a large window. It draws me close until I'm gazing out at the most gorgeous view. It's a clear view of the cliff—the land around the house, the growth of rock, and the spread of water. There's a plate with leftover lasagna. I'm guessing this is Mr. Rochester's office. He must have eaten here after we were done. How sad.

Why doesn't he join us?

The final door's at the end of the hallway. I turn the knob carefully, half expecting someone to appear. Mr. Rochester, most likely. It's dim. Empty. A stairwell.

Not a linen closet. I should move on to the other side of the house, but I'm drawn by the heat coming down through the narrow passageway. I'm drawn by curiosity. Sturdy wooden steps lead me to a finished attic. There's a metal bedframe in the corner, as if this was once used as a bedroom, but since then someone has added boxes and boxes of storage. There are shadows of old baby toys—a mechanical swing and a bouncer. They must have been Paige's.

This also feels private, but less grim than the room down there. These are people's heirlooms, their leftovers, the overflow of their lives. It does seem like if I found a blanket and pair of socks here, it would be fair for me to use them. After all, Mr. Rochester is supposed to provide room and board. Not freezing room and board, the regular kind.

That's how I justify it to myself as I start peeking into the boxes.

There doesn't seem to be much order to what's here. I find beautiful china in a box with old crayons and Legos. Paintings stacked against an old row boat. There's a journal lined with blue velvet that's soft to the touch and missing the layer of dust over everything else.

A creak in the wood from behind me.

I drop the journal and turn just as a hand grabs my wrist.

My scream pierces the darkness.

Mr. Rochester looks down at me, his eyes fierce, his face glowing from the light of his phone. "What the fuck are you doing up here?"

"I'm sorry," I say, instinctive panic making me desperate. It's more than just fear of losing my job. It's the reality of being in a tight space with an angry man. This hasn't ended well for me before. I'm rambling because I'm nervous. "I'm so sorry. I didn't know."

"That's not an answer."

"A blanket," I say, stumbling over the sylla-

41

bles. "And socks. I'm cold."

He looks incredulous, as if he hasn't noticed that it's twenty degrees outside. His dark gaze takes me in all the way down to my bare legs, to my feet, my freezing toes. "You're looking for a blanket. In a goddamn attic? Nothing is usable here."

"Is there… a linen closet somewhere?"

He growls, the sound animalistic in the small space. "Why didn't you tell me?"

"Why didn't you come to dinner?" I really have no right to demand answers of this man.

It's just an automatic reaction to his tone.

In the twenty-four hours since I met Beau Rochester, he's taken on a larger-than-life space in my mind. He seems taller than men should be, stronger than they usually are. Fiercer in every way.

It's a figment of my imagination, of course.

A side effect of meeting him in such a strange situation. But now that I see him standing over me, his chest bare, revealing muscles and a dark covering of hair, the gauzy light tracing the planes of his body, I realize it was accurate all along.

He shakes his head, still shocked about the whole cold situation. "You got here last night. Were you shivering in your room then, too?"

"Pretty much." Maybe I was exhausted by the plane ride and the kitten interview, because I eventually went to sleep. Though I was frozen solid when I woke up.

"There's this crazy thing called the Internet. Even here at the Coach House we can get deliveries from Amazon. Why didn't you just order something with same-day delivery?"

"Because someone threatened to fire me, and there's barely enough money in my bank account right now for a flight back to Houston until I get paid."

"Christ." He looks more furious than he should be for an employee being cold.

"Listen, if I found something that was clearly special—an embroidered baby cap or a wedding dress—I wasn't going to touch them. I just thought there might be a pile of blankets around. It seemed like those would be useful here in Maine."

"Ms. Mendoza. The attic is strictly off-limits to you. Do you understand?"

"Yes," I whisper.

"Follow me." He turns and stomps down the steps. I follow him more slowly, not eager for him to yell at me more or to return to my freezing room.

Mr. Rochester opens a door opposite mine. Inside I see a navy bedspread. It must be his room. He yanks the bedspread off and holds it up without a word. His brown eyes glint in the moonlight, sharp with demand or promise or something I'm afraid to name.

"I couldn't. It's *your* bedspread. If I take it, then you'll be cold."

"I went camping at Acadia National Park when I was ten. I won't die. You, however." He takes in my hard nipples and goose bump-covered legs in one dismissive glance. "I don't need the agency asking questions if you freeze to death."

"Is there maybe another room we could take it from?"

"No." The answer does not invite more questions.

"The room with the watch and the teacup? It's bigger than this one. The master bedroom." I look around the room, as small and bare as mine. "Why don't you sleep there?"

"You went in there? Jesus Christ."

"Let me guess. That one's forbidden too. Like the attic."

He makes a grunt in agreement.

Yes, sir. That's the only appropriate response, but something makes me ask. "That room's clearly the master bedroom. It's bigger than this one. Why don't you sleep there?"

"Leave it the fuck alone."

With a shivering hand I accept the blanket and clutch it against my chest. "Thank you."

He closes the door in my face.

What I didn't realize is that his bedspread would carry the faint musky scent of him. I close my eyes, but it doesn't go away. It only gets stronger. Now I know what it would be like to press my face against his chest. To be enclosed in a hug. I head back to my room. When I climb into bed, I pull the bedspread up and wrap it tightly around my body and fall into a deep slumber.

The next afternoon several packages arrive. There's a thick down comforter for my bed. There's also buttery soft socks, fur-lined boots, and a padded jacket.

I'm warm, finally, and it feels like bliss.

He doesn't ask for his bedspread back, and I don't offer it. I continue to sleep with the bedspread wrapped around me each night.

CHAPTER FIVE

W E SETTLE INTO an uneasy routine, spending most of our time caring for the kitten and lounging in the large rooms with Paige's favorite game in the world—Monopoly. She wants to play. And then she wants to play again. I go along with it, hoping that we're developing a rapport. The weather continues to be gloomy, so I don't force her to spend time outside. Which means she can continue to wear her clothes better suited to warmer climates.

I mention schoolwork to her a couple times a day, aiming for casual, hoping for cooperation. But whenever I bring up the subject, she shuts down completely.

Her one-word answers go to complete silence.

She walks away from the Monopoly board game and refuses to play.

Amidst some printed subtraction and fill-in-the-blank sentence worksheets, I find the login to the parent portal for her school.

A small icon shaped like an envelope has a little red number beside it. Fifty-one. There are fifty-one messages from her teacher, her principal, the administrator of the school.

Dear Mr. Rochester, We're so excited to be working with Paige. She's just a delight and so smart. We noticed she hasn't turned in her summer reading essay. Can you please contact Mrs. Temple so we can clear this up?

Dear Mr. Rochester, Unfortunately Paige missed her last two sessions of mathematics and science. She's in danger of falling behind. Of course her academic progress is of utmost importance. Please contact my office immediately.

Basically, if there was a principal's office, we'd all be inside right now.

It's not a typical public school where she attends each day. It's also not a typical homeschool where I create the curriculum. Instead it's like a private school using distance learning.

She has teachers, tests, grades—everything another first grade student would have.

But she does it on her own time. Or she's supposed to.

Dear Mr. Rochester, We are very concerned about Paige's many absences and her ability to catch up with the work required for her curriculum. Call the administrative office right away.

On a late Thursday afternoon, I leave Paige playing with the kitten, still unnamed, using a cat toy with a string on the end we ordered through the housekeeper. I use that time to step into the next room and call the school.

"Mrs. Rochester?" There's shuffling on the other end of the line. "Are you her mother?"

"No, no. I'm her nanny. I'm going to be working on her schoolwork with her."

"I don't see you here in this file."

"Oh, right. Yeah, I'm pretty new here. Just trying to figure out what she's supposed to be working on. I understand she's a little bit behind."

There's a muffled sound. Possible rude laughter stopped with a hand over her mouth. "A little behind? Paige is in danger of failing the first grade. Mrs. Rochester—"

"Uh, that's Ms. Mendoza. Or you know what? You can just call me Jane."

"Ms. Mendoza. Jane. I really would prefer to speak with Mr. Rochester—" More shuffling.

"Her uncle, is he? He and I spoke when she enrolled in the school, but he's been impossible to get in touch with since then. He's really the only one authorized to discuss her with us for privacy reasons."

"I understand." I can't exactly explain that Mr. Rochester has been impossible to get in touch with for me as well. In fact I haven't seen him since that night he caught me in the attic. It's almost as if he doesn't live in the mansion. "I'm sure he would love to speak with you about Paige. Her education is very important to him." This is a bold-faced lie, if the fifty-one unread messages are anything to go by. "But he's indisposed right now. If she has any hope of getting back on track for the year, basically I'm all you've got."

There's a pause. Then a sigh. "She's very far behind. In every subject. The only way she can catch up is by doing all the work she did not turn in."

I wince because I can't get her to talk about school. How am I going to get her to do an ordinary workload, much less a massive one full of make-up work? It's all well and good to shout "go do your homework" on a TV sitcom. It's another thing entirely when a grieving child who's lost her parents absolutely refuses to participate. There's no such thing as consequences in her world. I can't threaten to take away her board games or ground her from her friends, because the worst thing that can happen in her life has already happened.

We have that in common. I know exactly how she feels.

"We'll figure it out," I say, my tone sober. "Let me know where I can download all the work she needs to do, and we'll start submitting it. She's been having a really hard time."

"We here at Southminster are not uncaring of her situation."

"It's only been a few months since her parents passed away."

"If she were at a public school, it would be too late. She'd be held back for an entire year. Because of her enrollment with us—" In the pause, I understand what she means. Because she's wealthy enough to afford a private school tuition. "She has the chance to catch up. But she must do the work. We have an academic reputation to protect."

I hang up the phone and head back into the sitting room.

How am I supposed to convince Paige to do her schoolwork? I can put dinner on the table and wash her clothes. That's a different story than making her do schoolwork when she's determined to ignore it. The dilemma sits in my stomach like a stone the rest of the day. It floats in my body, hard and heavy, as I lay down in bed that night.

I lay there for hours—warm. Warm, because of Mr. Rochester's blanket. Full of questions, because of Mr. Rochester's secrets. He's not even in the room with me but he invades my body. He brushes across my surface and steals through my cracks.

Light flashes across the ceiling.

Lightning?

Or something else?

I sit up in bed and push the covers away. Cold air whispers underneath my nightgown and makes me shiver. I cross the room and look out the window. My stomach turns over from nerves. I'm trembling, but I force myself to search the grounds.

A full moon. Dark grass. An eternity of water peppered with white foam.

Rivulets of water distort the view, but I can see clearly enough. There's no one there. A shiver runs down my spine. Would I know if there was? There are so many trees. So much land. A million shadows. And frankly, the kitten is a terrible guard dog.

The night shifts, and I see someone walking. Tall. Broad shoulders. He could be any man, strong and large, but something about his gait tells me that it's Mr. Rochester. His looks straight ahead even as he walks over craggy, uneven rock, hands shoved into pockets. A white shirt has become dark and slick against his skin. The rain must be freezing. I'm cold, and I'm inside the house.

What is he doing out there?

He appears to be walking without a destination.

Why is he so distant with Paige? Some days I can tell he's trying his best to figure out Pop-Tarts and Monopoly when he never planned to be her parent. Other days I have less sympathy for him. It's not her fault her parents died.

There are moments I get the sense that he's hiding something. The feeling becomes stronger now, watching him. His shoulders are not hunched beneath the cold. It's like he can't sense the freezing rain. There's something much worse driving him. A tortured soul beneath muscle and bone.

Is he a monster who thinks of his niece with a balance sheet?

Or is he a broken man fighting a battle I don't

understand?

My heart squeezes. I pick up the blanket that he gave me. I'm loathe to give it back. It smells of him. Ridiculous, I know. It's been days. But he needs it more.

I run downstairs in my bare feet and fling open the door.

Rain pelts my skin, but I don't feel it. Maybe that's the way he is, driven by something deeper. The cold can't touch how badly I need to soothe him right now.

He blinks at me through water-logged lashes. "What the hell are you doing?"

"I'm giving you this." I hold out the blanket. It's wet. I'm also wet. This is ridiculous, but so is walking around the cliffside when it's slippery and freezing. "You'll catch your death."

His dark eyes look fierce in the moonlight. "It's no more than I deserve."

Unease runs through me. "What does that mean?"

"It means I'm not a good man, Jane. You shouldn't worry about me getting cold. The best thing that could happen is that I catch my death out here on these cliffs. It would be fitting."

It feels like he's punishing himself. That's why he's making himself walk in the freezing rain. It's why he won't accept help. "Don't talk like that."

He gives a short laugh. "You shouldn't care about me, Jane. You really shouldn't. One woman has already died. I wouldn't want that to happen to you."

Cold races over my arms. It has nothing to do with the rain. "Who? Paige's mom?"

"Go inside."

I hold out the blanket, which is heavy with rainwater. I can be stubborn, too. "Take it."

"You aren't paid to take care of me. You're paid to take care of Paige."

But you're hurting, I want to say. *You're hurting and grieving just as badly as she is. Maybe more.* His pain isn't as simple as missing his brother and his sister-in-law. There's something darker happening here. I feel its energy pulsing through the house. As if it's haunted, not with ghosts but with memories. "Come inside."

His gaze holds mine for an unbroken moment. In that time I see his pain. He means what he says. He feels responsible for someone's death. I'm not afraid of him, though.

Maybe that will be the death of me.

CHAPTER SIX

THE NEXT DAY after lunch I pull out her workbook. Pencils. Erasers. And a bright, fake smile that she can see right through. "We really need to do some schoolwork, Paige."

She continues sorting through the real estate cards. *St. James Place. Tennessee Avenue. New York Place.* Then, *Connecticut Avenue, Vermont Avenue, Oriental Avenue.* She likes grouping them. At first I thought it was a child's natural instinct to connect them by color. It didn't take me long after playing with her to realize it has more to do with strategy. When you have a monopoly on a single color, it becomes harder for the opponent (in other words, me) to avoid them. She can also build houses and hotels that way, making it more likely she'll bankrupt me in a single roll of the dice. The kitten has curled up to nap in the black plastic container that used to hold the small silver game markers.

"Paige? I know you don't like it, but we have

to do it."

"Why do I even need school?"

That's a tricky question. Because the law requires children to go to school. Because it's my job to make sure she does the work. Neither of those answers are likely to satisfy a defiant six year old. "So you can learn about the world around us."

That doesn't even earn me a glance. *Baltic Avenue. Mediterranean Avenue.* She can barely restrain her glee when she lands on one of those. Bloodthirsty little thing.

"I'm hungry," she says.

"We just ate."

"I'm still hungry."

There wasn't a large amount of the lobster stew today. The bowl is empty, and Mrs. Fairfax already left for the day. "Do you want a Pop-Tart?"

"No," she says, drawing out the word. "Mac and cheese."

"Okay." I'm no chef, but I can make this happen with a blue box. I head into the kitchen and pull out the butter, the milk. I'm heating up water in the pan when I peek back into the dining room. Empty. The real estate cards fan out on the table.

There's no Paige in sight. No kitten, either.

Shit. It's not the first time she's snuck from the room. She's quiet and stealthy, but usually I'm able to keep track of her. Aside from folding her laundry and organizing the papers for her schoolwork, it's my only job. Now she's gone.

Probably because I asked her to do school-work. This isn't a coincidence.

I head down the expansive hallway, peeking into each of the large sitting areas and come up empty. Hmm. Next I go upstairs to her room to see if she decided to curl up in bed.

Her room is empty.

The room next door that holds her desk—also empty.

I try a few of the doors since I'm up here and find only spare rooms like mine. A few of the doors are locked. And in one last, random attempt, I peek into my own room. Nope, no one here. I even check the bathroom, in case Paige brought the kitten here to use the litter box.

From here I can see through the window to the outside.

Rain comes down in thick, uneven droplets.

Where could she be?

In a terrible but necessary repeat, I check all the same places again. The room where I left her—this time, under the couch and behind the armoire. The other rooms, calling her name. The dining room. The kitchen.

"Kitten," I call in a high voice. "Kitten, where are you?"

Paige has refused to name the kitten, and I can't do it since I already offered her the privilege. So the kitten is called kitten. Sometimes she meows when you call her that.

Silence. It's like I'm in the house alone.

A shiver runs down my spine.

I go upstairs again and check her bedroom, her school room, my bedroom. I even check the strange bedroom with the watch and teacup— empty. I break the rules and check the attic. Nothing.

Finally, in desperation, I reach Mr. Rochester's study door.

I hear a low voice coming through. "There's no way I can make it to check the building myself. I don't care how important it is. It's not happening. I'm stuck here in goddamn Maine on a goddamn life raft, because it doesn't ever stop raining. So you and the rest of those lawyers getting paid five hundred dollars an hour will just have to do your fucking jobs and figure it out."

I knock on the ornately carved door and open.

He turns to face me. "What?" he asks, brusque and annoyed.

"Have you seen Paige?" I ask, knowing that he'll censure me for losing track of her. And worse, he should censure me. I know better than to leave her alone for even a minute. An ordinary six-year-old girl? Sure. She could survive on her own while you make mac and cheese. One reeling from loss and angry at the world? That's a different story.

"You don't know where she is?" he asks, slamming his phone on the desk. "You misplaced her like a sock in the goddamn dryer? Please explain to me what I'm paying you for."

"Listen. You can be angry at me, you can hate me. You can fire me, but right now I just need to find her. So I'm assuming you haven't seen her. I'll keep looking."

He lets out a growl of frustration and follows me through the hallway and down the stairs. "Did you check the living room with the fireplace? She likes to hide underneath the chairs there."

"Already checked."

"What about the pantry? Those Pop-Tarts—"

"I came from the kitchen. She's not there."

"Her room? She can slip away and end up taking a nap."

I whirl on him. "So what you're saying is that you already know she has a habit of sneaking away and hiding, and you didn't bother to warn me about it?"

He looks grim. "I thought it was only me she'd hide from."

The innate sadness of that statement makes my heart clench. But the unease I've been feeling at her absence turns into acute worry. The fact that she has a history of hiding makes it clear she's an expert at this. Maybe she's decided to try a new hiding spot.

I glance again at the windows. "What if she went outside?"

"It's freezing out there."

"She's—" My voice breaks. "She's hurting. She's beyond hurting. She's numb with it. When you're grieving like that, you can't feel physical pain the same way."

He gives me a grim look before turning to the window. "Then we'll check outside. If there's a chance she's out there, we need to bring her inside before she gets sick."

Our eyes meet, and in his dark gaze I see the haunting knowledge of his concern for her. He may be in over his head with this whole business of raising a little girl, but he does care about her.

There's stark fear in his eyes that he might fail her. It makes my heart squeeze.

We head to the front door, grabbing our jackets that hang by the door. I slip my worn-out Converse knockoffs onto my bare feet and head outside.

Without saying words we agree to split up and search in opposite directions. I head to the left and he heads to the right. I tromp over the uneven ground, slipping a couple of times. Even with the dim light of evening, it's hard to get around.

Each drop of water that hits me feels like a slap in the face.

I keep going.

As I near the cliff, it turns into pure rock. I get this strange feeling as I walk closer, this sense that I'm testing the knife's edge of my mortality. One slip, and I'd go over. One fall, and I'd break my neck. I don't have the luck or the nine lives of a kitten. If I fell forty feet, I would die.

Morbid fear has me creeping closer so I can peek over the edge. In a moment of panic, I can almost imagine seeing her—a small broken body at the bottom where the water meets rock. The flash of red and black, the colors she loves to wear.

There's nothing down there.

I pull myself back and continue walking along the water line. In the distance I can see mist covering a red lighthouse. I wonder if Paige can see it from where she is right now.

"Paige," I call, though the wind whips my voice away to nothing. I keep shouting for her until I turn hoarse. Then I start making little kissy sounds for the kitten. "Kitten. Where are you?"

A meow trickles through the air.

I whip my head to the right, wondering if I imagined it.

"Kitten? Paige! Where are you?"

The meow comes again, and I start running, slipping and sliding over the terrain to get to her. I find her sitting in a forlorn little pile at the foot of a tree. I glance around, anxious to see Paige. Nothing. A faint crack comes from above. I look up and see her skirt hanging off a branch about ten feet off the ground.

"Oh my God. Paige. Are you okay?"

She peeks over the edge, her expression torn between anger and fear. It's not a coincidence that she ran away while I was on the phone with her school. She must have overheard me. "I don't need your help. I don't need anyone. Just leave me alone."

"God, you must be freezing. How long have

you been out here? This whole time?"

Quiet sobbing is the only answer. It would be easy to be angry at a child for being disobedient. I saw it often enough in the foster homes where I lived. It's much harder to deal with the pain underneath. And she has so much pain.

Immediately I can see how this will play out. If I demand she come down, she'll respond exactly the way she did when Mr. Rochester insisted she put on a jacket and pants. If I go get Mr. Rochester, he might drag her down—but ten feet off the ground, I'm not even sure he could retrieve her safely if she's fighting him.

I take off my jacket and wrap it around the kitten so she's safe on the ground. Then I begin to climb. This kind of tree doesn't grow back in Houston where I lived before. I don't even know what it's called. Pine? Fir? It's some kind of giant Christmas tree, basically. There's a very small protruding branch about five feet off the ground. It probably supported Paige, no problem. It cracks ominously under my weight. The trunk of the tree leaves a gash on my forearm and sticks something sharp into my ankle, but I manage to make it onto the branch opposite her.

"What are you doing?" she asks, her voice watery.

"Sitting with you."

"Don't you want me to come down?"

"Well, yes. It is cold. And I care about you. I didn't think you'd want to come down right away, though, and if you're going to be out here, then I'll keep you company."

"It doesn't matter," she says. "You don't know what it's like."

"Try me."

"You're just like *him*. You want me to eat broccoli and do my homework and be a good girl, but what does it even matter? Huh? It means nothing. *He* gets to walk around outside at night, but I have to be trapped in that house."

"You're right," I say, my voice softer and shivering—whether it's the cold or the starkness of the emotions, I'm a mess right now. "I do want you to eat broccoli and do your homework. One day those things will be important to you, too, but not right now. I get that."

"No, you don't."

"It feels like nothing matters now that your parents are gone. It feels like there's no reason for living. Or worse—like maybe if you'd just been better while they were alive, if you'd brushed your teeth without them having to ask you, if you'd gotten a better grade at school, maybe they'd still be alive. But they wouldn't. They wouldn't. And it feels like it will never be okay again."

There's more crying. "Yes. *Yes.*"

Something shifts in the trees beyond us, and I realize that Mr. Rochester has found us. He's letting me talk to her, though, and I'm grateful for that.

"I do know, sweetheart. My dad died when I was twelve. Older than you, but he was still my whole world. And it hurt so bad. Worse than the time I broke my arm. Worse than anything I could imagine. I felt like I was bleeding, like I was dying inside, and no one could see that. They thought I was fine. They thought I could just be sad and then move on."

A sniffle now. "What did you do?"

"I don't know. Or maybe I do know, I just don't want you to copy my example. I went dead inside, really. I just pretended like I was okay, but I wasn't okay. Not then, and not now. Maybe I never will be, but I don't want that for you, sweetheart. You aren't a ward of the state. You have a family. You have a home. You can feel safe again, someday."

"It's not a real home," she says, her voice thick. This is not the child full of anger and resentment. There's only sadness now. "It's not a real family."

"It may not seem like Mr. Rochester cares about you, but he does."

"He doesn't."

"I care about you, too."

"You don't either. I heard Beau talk to you on the first day. I'm the reason why you're getting a paycheck right now. That's why you're here. Because of money."

The accusation draws blood because it's true. "Yes. I can't deny that."

"See? No one cares about me anymore."

"Do you know the reason why I accepted this job? Why I moved so far away from where I lived? Because I want to go to college and become a social worker. Because I want to help kids, kids like you who've gone through something hard. I may have only met you because I took the job, but now that I'm here and I've gotten to know you, I do care about you. Only for you." I swallow hard around the knot in my throat, knowing I might very well get fired after this. "And no matter what happens, even if I have to go away, I will never stop caring about you."

I know the birthday and favorite food of every kid who was ever a foster child in a home with me. Even the ones who stole lunch money from my backpack, even the ones who got me in trouble to save their own skins. They're all part of my broken, haunting family.

And now there's Paige.

And somehow, *somehow* there's Mr. Rochester.

She sniffles. "I'm still not going to do the schoolwork. It still doesn't matter."

I drop my head back against the rough bark. "I understand."

"We can go inside though. Can I have a Pop-Tart?"

An uneven laugh escapes me. "Sure, sweetheart."

Boots crunch across twigs on the ground. Mr. Rochester appears, looking sober and severe. Without a word, he reaches his arms up for Paige. She's still a good three feet above him. Her feet dangle out of reach. I hold my breath.

She lifts her arms and then lets herself fall. He catches her easily, like her forty-five pounds is nothing at all. My hands clench at the branch I'm on. There's trust between them, even if they're both denying it. Even if they're both grieving separately. It was clear in that single jump, where she left the branch and landed in his arms, knowing he would be there.

I don't have that kind of safety net.

Grasping the top of the branch, I swing myself down so I'm hanging by my palms. The bark rips into my skin, leaving broken streaks of blood all the way down. I let myself go and fall onto the hard-packed ground. Shocks of pain shoot up my calves.

Mr. Rochester turns and walks away, carrying Paige in his arms.

I scoop up the kitten and carry her inside the mansion for the second time.

When we make it inside the door, Mr. Rochester sets Paige down and points toward the kitchen. "Get yourself a Pop-Tart and put it in the toaster. I'll be in there in a minute to start it. And I might even make you some hot chocolate."

She runs off without a backward glance. Children are in that strange place, where everything impacts them deeply, cuts linger for the rest of their lives. But they're also resilient.

He turns to me when we're alone. "Head upstairs."

"I can get her the hot chocolate," I say, licking my dry lips.

That earns me a dark look. "You're a mess. Head upstairs. Clean yourself up."

I look down and confirm that he's right. I

look fairly grotesque with my hands cut to ribbons. That doesn't even count the way my ankle feels taut and swollen beneath my jeans. "I'm sorry about losing track of her."

"We'll talk when you aren't covered in blood."

I climb the stairs with the kitten in tow and set her down in her litterbox, which she uses right away. Ironically she's probably been holding it sitting outside.

Don't think about it. There's a deluge forming against a dam. It's been building for a long, long time. I've never really talked about my father's death. I avoided the topic, and if it came up, I'd say, "It was a long time ago." Which is bullshit, really. It's like I told Paige up in that tree. *I just pretended like I was okay, but I wasn't okay. Not then, and not now.* I never got over his death. And I never will. Society gives us timetables. Oh, you can be sad for this much time. And you can be angry for a little bit here. But then you move on.

What does moving on look like? What does it even mean?

I lost my father, my guardian, my entire family that day. There is no *next* for me.

My wet clothes fall into a soggy heap on the white tile. I step beneath the burning spray of the shower. It stings from where my skin has gone chilled and numb. Sometimes it's worse to feel anything at all. I lean back and slide down the wall to the floor. There's no tomorrow. College. A job. *It still doesn't matter.* Paige was right about that.

I cover my face with my bloody hands and cry.

CHAPTER SEVEN

A FIRE CRACKLES in the hearth. It sounds real. It looks real. It probably feels hot to the touch, but I'd bet it's one of those gas fireplaces. Or maybe electric. With those logs made out of ceramic and sculpted to look like wood. No actual branches burn here.

I take a painful step into the room. Another.

Firelight traces the stark planes of his face, making him look more severe. He does not turn when I come into the room. Nor when I sit in the armchair opposite him. If he's going to fire me, I might as well be seated in this plush leather cushion while he does it.

"Hi," I say.

He casts a sardonic look my way. "How are your hands?"

"Fine," I lie, even though they're burning. I don't bother showing them, because they'd only disprove the point. They don't even compare to how much my ankle hurts. Thankfully he didn't watch me walk in with a limp. "I took a couple Advil, so I feel better."

He doesn't seem like he believes me. He also doesn't seem like he cares that much. His sherry-colored eyes manage to look cold. "So, your parents died when you were a child as well?"

I flinch. Maybe I should have expected this line of questioning. I knew he heard me talking to Paige, but I assumed he'd fire me and be done with it. "Yes."

After taking a shower I joined them down-stairs to find that Mr. Rochester had already prepared an early dinner for his niece. Mac and cheese from a blue Kraft box, along with a Pop-Tart for dessert. He informed me that he'd help her get ready for bed. I was to wait and meet him in his study at nine p.m. Now she's asleep. Now, for all intents and purposes, we're alone.

Hanging from that branch with the bark digging into my palms felt better than this.

"You were older than Paige is now."

"Older when my father died. Younger when my mother died."

"A sad story." I've received plenty of sympathy over the years. Fake sympathy, mostly. The kind Paige got from the school principal. *I'm sorry, but you need to get over it.* This is different. Mr.

Rochester does not offer sympathy. He remarks, as if on the weather.

"Are you going to fire me?"

He considers me, unmoved by my question. It's not that he's saying yes or saying no. He does not feel compelled to answer me. "And after that. You had no family to take you in?"

"My mother's parents are still alive. They refused."

"Why?"

"For the same reason they disowned her when she married my dad, probably."

"Which was?"

"His race. His lack of money. Whatever the reason, they didn't explain it to me." My father was from Mexico. An undocumented immigrant, technically, though he was naturalized when he was young. My own citizenship has never been in question since I was born here, but I've faced plenty of dirty looks, discrimination, and muttered comments to go back where I came from over the years.

With my dark hair, dark eyes, and olive skin, I look like my father.

The irony is I've never traveled out of the United States. I don't speak any Spanish. I know as much about Mexican culture as my mother, who was white. My father was too busy working long hours at a call center to teach me about it. He was more concerned that I ace English literature than learn Spanish. On the rare nights he got home before eight p.m. we'd order pizza delivery and watch Battle Bots together.

When he died I lost more than a father. More than a family.

I lost my only link to that half of my heritage.

He picks up a file on the side table. It sat there all this time, being an innocuous manila folder. Now he pulls it onto his lap and opens it, it becomes something else. A grainy picture of me as a child sits on top, a serious expression because I never smiled even when my father was alive. A serious child, everyone said. Other people would insist that I should smile, but Daddy would stop them. "No, she'll smile when she wants to. Not before."

Mr. Rochester rifles through the pages. "I confess I didn't look this over very carefully before you were hired. I read the references you sent. The one by your social worker. Very nice. The one by your current boss at the store. Excellent. A couple families where you did occasional babysitting. Everything seemed stellar, and the agency itself came highly recommended, so I considered it enough. Why would I need to know your entire life story?"

"You don't."

He gives me a half smile. "It's interesting reading, I've come to find out. The straight A student. You never had a problem with turning in your work. Even when your father died, you kept on getting straight As. Valedictorian of your middle school and high school."

"Everyone grieves differently."

"That's true. Paige Rochester attempts to freeze to death."

His scornful tone makes a knot form in my chest. "And how do you grieve, Mr. Rochester? By acting like an asshole to your niece? It was your brother, after all."

"And my sister-in-law. Don't forget her."

I stand up. "If you're going to be disrespectful to the deceased—"

"Sit down, Ms. Mendoza."

"They were your family. She is your family. They deserve better than to be—"

"I said, sit down." He doesn't raise his voice. He doesn't have to. I sit down. "You know nothing about my family. A few days with a rebellious child doesn't give you a decade's worth of secrets and lies."

"I don't need to know your secrets or your lies. I already know that little girl is hurting, and you aren't helping her nearly enough."

"Agreed."

I open my mouth to continue my tirade before realizing what he's said. "You agree?"

"Yes. I've known that I was too distant. Too abrupt. Too much of an asshole, to use your terminology. I thought getting a nanny would help, and the truth is, it has. You brought her down from that tree a lot quicker and painlessly than I would have."

"Oh. Thanks."

He continues paging through the manila folder. Apparently admitting you're an asshole doesn't make you actually stop the behavior.

Sure, I signed papers agreeing to every kind of background check imaginable. I did a blood draw and peed in a cup for the Bassett Agency, but he wasn't interested in those things before hiring me. He's only curious now because he wants to humiliate me.

And the worst part is, it's working. It's a cold churn in my stomach.

"It says here that you work at a diner. And a grocery store." His gaze challenges me, dares me to tell him it's none of his damn business.

"I did, yes. Before coming here." I hope I can get my jobs back if he does fire me, but there's no guarantee. He may have complimented me a second ago, but he's mercurial enough not to care. If I displease him, I'll be gone. I know that much is true.

"The agency called the grocery store manager, your shift manager, and someone named Noah Palmer. He works with you. According to this, you've known him for years."

My cheeks burn. "We were in the same foster home."

"Coincidence?"

"I worked at the diner through high school. After I graduated I needed another job, and he knew they had an opening at the cheese counter."

"Gouda," he says. "Camembert. I do enjoy a good manchego."

"It's really not that kind of grocery store. They sell mostly mozzarella and cheddar. My job was to clean out the slicer between slicing the meats and the cheeses."

"Why are you here?"

I glance back at the dark hallway. And then toward the fire. "You told me. You told me nine o'clock in your study."

"Not here in this room. You could have been

in the city where you grew up, selling mozzarella and cheddar. With your family." He corrects himself. "With your friends. Instead you decided to move to the coldest, wettest place on earth. I want to know why."

"You have my whole life written down in black and white right in front of you."

"It doesn't tell me anything about what's going on in that pretty little head of yours. Did you think you'd hook up with the playboy Beau Rochester and get your picture in the tabloids? Precious little of that here in Eben Cape."

My pulse speeds up. "What are you talking about?"

"Are you really saying you've never seen me on the news before?"

"I have no idea what you're talking about, but if you want to look in those pages so badly, look at my course load. All AP classes. Look at my hours at the diner and then at the grocery store. When would I have time to look up news articles about some random guy in Maine?"

He gives me a cynical smile, though I sense the derision is directed more at himself. "I didn't always hide in the corner of the country. At one time I made more money than one man can ever spend in a lifetime—but I sure did try."

"Doing what?" A memory of the drive up the mountain slams into me like a gust of wind. I remember seeing the wild sea. "Fishing?"

A bark of laughter. "You really have never heard of me."

"Who are you?"

"Nobody. Absolutely fucking nobody."

I glare at him. "Don't mock me."

He smiles. "I created a company. I didn't really give a flying shit about shipping, but I saw there was an opening. It's basically an Uber for commercial purposes. I didn't care; just wanted the money. And I made it. That's the dream, isn't it? Make billions. Show the cheerleader back in high school that she missed out by not sucking my dick."

"You're disgusting."

"If you think every man who tries to get rich doesn't think about that, you're fooling yourself. And I'm sure more than one man has imagined you that way."

"I was no cheerleader."

"No, but every boy who saw those lips thought the same thing that I do. You probably scurried through the high school halls, your books pressed to your chest to try to hide the fact that you were becoming a woman, but they could tell anyway, couldn't they?"

I shift to stand up, but he's somehow already in front of me. He looks down at me from above. I can't see his expression. The firelight draws him in deep charcoal. My heart beats faster. I should be afraid of the way he's standing over me, afraid of the way he's blocking my only exit. Other men have done this. Other men have hurt me. I don't want him to hurt me, but I want him to touch me. It's a strange sensation. Something about hearing him say the word *woman* in relation to my body. I'm not a woman, not really. I'm something before that. A bud all tight and green and white, only the faintest hint of pink at the tip. That's me. And he's the heat from the sun, drawing me open. I look up at him, waiting to see what he'll do next.

And what he does is run a finger across my jaw.

I shiver in the warm room.

It's such a soft touch. A cannonball across the boundaries of what's allowed between an employer and his employee, between the man of the house and the nanny. I hold my breath, waiting for him to tell me what to do. That seems like the real reward of this man, the upside of dealing with his meanness, that he will tell me what to do. Not like Noah, who looks and looks and looks. He wants me, but he doesn't know any more than I do.

Mr. Rochester touches lightly along my shoulder. He reaches down to pick up my two hands, palms up. They look dark and gruesome in the firelight. The bleeding stopped after my shower, but the scabs look ugly. "These must hurt," he murmurs.

"I don't feel them," I whisper. All I can feel is his hands holding mine from beneath.

"Because you're hurting. Isn't that right? You're beyond hurting. You're numb with it."

That's what I told him earlier. *When you're grieving like that, you can't feel physical pain the same way.* And it's true. For years I've lived in this ice-cold space. He's the only person who makes me feel anything. I want more of it even as I shrink away.

He lets my hands drop to my lap and walks out of the room.

CHAPTER EIGHT

MY RELATIONSHIP WITH Paige Rochester blossoms after the day in the tree. We still spend most of our time playing with the kitten or playing Monopoly, but she's way more willing to share her thoughts with me. She chatters endlessly about the characters in her game and makes up little songs about the kitten, who still goes by the name Kitten.

On a day when the weather is clear, we take a long hike down to the nearby beachfront shops in Newport, where we explore a coffee shop that sells empanadas in their bakery case, a fancy chocolatier with truffles shaped like little animals, and a toy store with an elaborate paper origami dinosaur flying beneath the sign.

We step inside, and the woman who runs it greets Paige.

"What do you love?" she asks.

"Colors," Paige says. "Lots and lots of colors."

And so she takes us to the side entrance where

there are fairy gardens and a large selection of painted river rocks. We go home with a large case of paints and paintbrushes. Soon, there are more rocks inside the house than outside. She covers them in black railroads and red parking meters, blue treasure chests and an orange jail, complete with a "just visiting" section.

The problem is her schoolwork.

Whenever I bring it up, she shuts down completely. Stops what she's doing, folds her little arms across her chest, and refuses to speak to me. For hours.

Unfortunately, it's very effective. No amount of arguing, pleading, or commanding changes her behavior. I can't even get her to *look* at the printed pages.

I have no means of forcing her to do the work, no way of disciplining her—not to mention, I'm not sure punishment would be the correct action to take for a grieving child.

Searching online I find that the problem is common for children who have undergone such trauma in their lives. It has nothing to do with her ability to understand the work. In fact, all signs point to the fact that she has an above average intelligence. She got As in kindergarten and can already read full sentences. She's curious, industrious, and smart, but she's going to flunk the first grade if something doesn't change. And fast.

After giving a sleepy Paige a kiss on the forehead, I go to his study.

I knock, and Mr. Rochester looks up from his papers. A lamp throws his face into hard relief, making him look severe. Or maybe that's just him.

"Come in," he says, and I step into the room. I'm glad we aren't in the narrow hallway again. I can still feel the echo of his touch under my chin and down my arms.

That was a strange night. It must have been some culmination of our fear for Paige. Or maybe it was because of the scratches on my hands which have begun to heal in uneven scabs.

It's not something that will ever happen again, basically.

I'm carrying some of Paige's unfinished schoolwork. He nods toward one of the armchairs in front of his desk, and I sit down. With the large slab of wood between us, this feels much more like an interview than the night with the kitten.

"The good news is that I'm getting along great with Paige. She's even started wearing pants and a hoodie when we go outside to collect rocks. But with schoolwork, we really aren't getting very far. She completely shuts down if I even mention it."

He leans back in his chair. His eyes reflect the lamp, the room, even me—they share nothing of what he's thinking. Of course, I can assume it isn't good. "It's part of your job to make sure she does her schoolwork, is it not?"

"Yes," I say, swallowing hard.

I'm sitting here with a stack proving my failure right now. Half an inch thick of worksheets and maps and graphs empty of a six-year-old's scribbles.

I just don't know what to do. This wasn't covered in the first aid training the Bassett Agency paid for me to take. I never had to do virtual learning with my foster siblings. Even in their most angry phases, I only had to get them onto the bus. It was the school's issue from that point on.

I've become the bus driver, teacher, and principal all at once.

My voice is wavery as I attempt a defense. "I don't know if this could have been avoided. Maybe it's part of her grieving process, but I would like to point out that there are months of incomplete work. This wasn't something new that happened when I arrived."

He gives me a sardonic glance. "Yes, it turns out she did not quite appreciate my teaching style. All the students who took my seminar at Yale surely agree with her. That's why I hired you. To teach her in a way that works for her."

"I don't think this is an issue of teaching style. She refuses to even talk about school."

"There's nothing to talk about. You put the work in front of her, and she does it."

I shake my head helplessly. "She doesn't."

"Are you asking for my permission to beat her? Permission granted, I think. A few hard straps of leather, and she'd change her tune."

I can't tell whether he's joking or not. "That's not funny."

A ghost of a smile. "I didn't think so at the time either. Effective, though."

"I'm not going to spank her." *And you shouldn't either,* I add silently. The last thing that grieving child needs from her only remaining family member is physical pain.

"Maybe you'll take a ruler to the backs of her fingers. I imagine that'll work just as well. And it will have the side benefit of giving me something nice to look at. You wearing a prim skirt and heels, a bun in your hair, wielding a ruler would be a sight to see."

My mouth opens. He may not be joking, but he's not serious either. This is a decided effort to rile me up, and it's working. "You're an asshole."

A quirk of his lips. "What do you want me to say?"

"That you're concerned about her education."

"Fuck her education."

"She's going to fail first grade. That will follow her the rest of her life."

He glances at the stack of papers. "Let me see that."

I hand it over. He looks at a page of simple three-letter sight words. "She can already read."

"I know." That's easy enough if you watch her play her games. She also snuck a look at my text messages one time. *Who is Noah and why does he want you to call him back?* "She's still supposed to draw lines from the words in butterflies to the flowers where they belong."

"Christ." He turns the page. From here I can see the giant circles forming a caterpillar that have giant numbers in them. "She can already do addition."

"And subtraction." It only took one time playing Monopoly with her before I realized she had the mind of a landlord. She could calculate the amount of rent due with two houses before I even realized I'd landed on her property. "She still needs to write the sum at the end of the caterpillar. It's not a question of how smart she is; it's about doing the work."

"The work is a joke."

"She's six."

"Even more reason she shouldn't be made to endure this pedestrian drivel."

"Listen, she's not a duchess being forced to mingle with the masses. She's a child who's hurting and needs something more from you than a rude remark."

He gives me a grin. It's sudden and unexpected, that flash of white teeth. He looks almost... handsome when he does that. As quickly as it appears, it's gone. "You would make an excellent schoolteacher," he murmurs, looking down my body with appreciation. "I've seen videos that start this way. And you could probably earn more than being a nanny."

Only then do I realize that I'm standing. Both my hands are on his desk, and I'm attempting to loom over him to help make my point. I sit down—hard.

Porn. He means porn.

Heat suffuses my cheeks, but I've lost all of my indignancy. Is he flirting with me? Or mocking me?

He leans forward. His hands steeple. "This is simple. You do the work."

I stare at him. Is this another one of his crude jokes? "Excuse me?"

He glances down. "Here, you draw a line between this bee and this flower. And here on this worksheet, you add up these numbers and put the answer in the caterpillar's asshole. They've got a real garden theme going on here, don't they?"

"I can't do the work for her."

"I see your point," he says, turning the page. "This coloring page is going to really stretch you. Color all the ladybugs that have a number less than ten. I mean, which way do you go? Realism? A nice red with black dots? Or do you go with other colors?"

"I can't do the work because it's hers."

"Do you think the teacher's going to figure it out? Maybe you should get one of the caterpillar ass numbers wrong just to be safe."

I glare at him. "It's not ethical."

"Life's not ethical, sweetheart. Or haven't you figured that out yet?"

I hate that I know what he means. Going to sleep hungry so the children could be fed, giving money to the bullies so I could walk away relatively unharmed. Other people my age are going to college with a nice fund maybe supplemented with a few loans. Their parents are driving them to the dorm rooms, trunks full of new sheets and dishes from Ikea. I don't want to become bitter about it, but it hurts. God, sometimes it just hurts to keep going.

"It will teach her the wrong thing," I whisper. "She knows she has this work piled up. If it suddenly goes away, if she finds out that I did it, she'll learn the wrong thing."

"And the butterflies and caterpillars are teaching her the right thing?"

"It's better than lying."

"I built a billion-dollar company before I turned thirty. Do you think I did that by coloring in the lines? By filling out little worksheets? The world doesn't give a fuck about first grade."

"Then what about next year? She'll be behind."

"Because she won't know about writing inside caterpillars? She already knows how to read and count and add numbers. She doesn't need the fucking cuteness."

"I'm not the one who set the curriculum. The school did. The school *you* picked."

His nostrils flare. Dark emotion flashes

through his eyes. "She's already lost her parents, because of me. *Because of me.* I'm not going to make her do a fucking butterfly just so I can give myself a pat on the back about her goddamn education."

I blink, taken aback by his outburst. It's maybe the first real thing he's ever said to me. I realize this is not only about her grief. It's about his. "Why would you say it's because of you?"

He tosses the papers back at me, and I have to jump quickly to catch them before they fly around the room. "Do the work," he mutters. "Make her do it. Make the crows outside do it. See if I fucking care who does the worksheet, but get her to pass first grade—or get on a plane back to Houston and say goodbye to your salary."

CHAPTER NINE

I WAKE SUDDENLY, sitting up in the dark, sweating.

Something happened. A dream? I can't remember anything. Only blackness.

The moon hangs high in my window. I peek at my phone. Two thirty a.m. There are a couple unread texts from Noah from our last conversion. *Don't do it*, he says. *It's a fucking trap. The rich people trap. They get people like us to do their work for them.*

It's not like that, I type back with a swipe of my finger. *It's not about money.*

He should be asleep, especially with an early shift at the grocery store tomorrow morning. But he replies back right away. *It's always about money.*

I lie back down, wondering what woke me up. I keep my phone on silent, so it wasn't his texts. The ocean rumbles outside, beating against the cliffside like a drum. It's a soothing noise. Nothing that would startle me.

A sound comes, a sharp cry.

I sit up again and slide my feet to the freezing cold wooden floor.

By the time the sound comes again I'm already stepping into the hallway. A light comes on a few doors away, and I take a small step back. Mr. Rochester emerges from his room looking rumpled and sleepy and somehow more human than ever before. He's wearing a plain white T-shirt that hugs muscles I've already seen. The plaid flannel pajama pants hang low.

He enters Paige's room, and her crying quiets.

I'm not sure why I don't just enter the room and announce myself, but I find myself creeping forward. Maybe I want to see what they're like together, without me in the middle. Or maybe I want to give him a chance to build a rapport with her. He may have been fighting with her tooth and nail before I arrived, over Pop-Tarts and sweaters, but at least he had a relationship.

Now he mostly manages to avoid her.

"What's wrong?" he says, his voice low. "Did you have the dream again?"

A sniffle. "It was different this time."

"Do you want to tell me about it?"

Silence, where I can imagine her shaking her head *no*.

"Do you think you can go back to sleep?"

"I'm afraid," the small voice says, and my heart wrenches. This is the part that Noah doesn't understand. Grief does not care whether you're rich or poor.

It hurts us equally.

I step into the room then, and Mr. Rochester's head half-turns to see me. "Do you want Ms. Mendoza to sit with you?"

There's another wrench in my heart. Because he sounds so uncertain. It's clear in this moment that whatever asshole things he says to me, he does care about this little girl.

"I want you both," she says, so I sit down on the floor against the wall. I leave him to be the one to smooth her hair back from her forehead and check if she has enough water by her bedside.

She's a small lump under the covers.

He sits on the edge of the bed.

"Do you want me to read a book to you?"

She shakes her head.

"Are you sure? I can pull something up on my Kindle. Investing Common Stocks or Fundamentals of Index Funds. I can have you asleep in minutes."

She giggles. "No, Uncle Beau."

"Then what should we talk about?"

"Mama used to sing to me," she says, her

voice shy.

There's a long silence, and I tense, knowing that Beau Rochester has a thousand sharp words in his mouth. He could slice her to ribbons without meaning to. "A song, huh?"

She nods.

"I'm not sure I even remember how to sing," he says slowly. "It's been a long time since I sang anything at all. What would your mother sing to you?"

"Taylor Swift."

He lets out a low laugh. "I definitely don't know the words to her songs."

"Well then, what songs *do* you know?"

I eye him dubiously. What kind of music does a man like Mr. Rochester listen to? Hard rock? Heavy metal? It matches his intensity, but I can't quite imagine him rocking out. Maybe something more adult. Classical music. Opera? That would fit his wealth and this outrageous mansion, but he seems too primitive to appreciate those things.

Maybe it's the water banging against the rocks that's his music. Something elemental.

"There was a light far away," his voice comes low and soothing. "I followed the water's gift. But when the night turned to day, I ended up adrift."

"What's that from?" she asks.

"An old fishing song." He murmurs the answer as if sharing a confession. "Our father was a lobsterman. He would come home and dance with our mother around the room."

"Here?" Paige asks, clearly entranced with this story. Apparently she knows as little family history as I do, judging by her excitement.

"In this house? No. It was a small thing, our house, almost falling down. Every Sunday he'd be outside nailing some boards somewhere, as if he put the whole thing together again."

"Did you ever go out on the boat?"

"Oh yes. You don't have two strapping sons without putting them to work. I spent most Saturday mornings on the boat with him." His voice turns teasing. "Can't eat lobster to this day. Have seen just about enough of them to suit me."

She giggles. "Is that why you didn't become a lobsterman?"

"No." He looks toward the moon. "There were other reasons for that."

"Sing more," she says, tugging him back to the present.

And so he does, his low voice filling the room. It's melodic and earthy, both a song to match the stride of work as well as a song to lull someone to sleep. "When I saw the light again, I knew it was a dream. But when the sky began to rain, there was the lighthouse gleam."

He continues singing about a man lost at sea, wandering through the ocean, drunk on the salt-spray, delirious with dreams of finding land. Paige's eyes flutter closed, and then open, and then closed again. Soon she becomes still in the way of sleep. It's just as well that she doesn't hear the ending to the song. The sailor never does find his way home.

Instead he's swallowed by the sea.

As the last note drifts into silence, I stand up quietly and step out of the room.

Mr. Rochester joins me in the hallway and closes the door.

"That's a sad song," I whisper. We're still standing two feet away from her room. I don't want to wake her up again, but it feels like a night for confidences.

"It's a sad life, fishing."

"Is that why you didn't become a lobster-man?"

"No, that's not why. For a long time I thought that's what I would do. And then I—" A soft laugh. "Well, isn't it always this way? I fell in love with a woman."

"She didn't like lobsters."

"She didn't like being poor. So I set out to become rich."

"It worked." I'm not just saying that because he lives in a fancy house or pays a high salary to a nanny. I'm not only saying it because he mentioned selling a billion-dollar business. I looked him up after he asked if I had seen him in the news.

And sure enough, there are plenty of references about Beau Rochester.

"You looked me up," he says.

"Yes." Some of them appear in magazines like Forbes and Wired, in articles about his company, about the new age of tech business, and how it's revolutionizing the old guard of shipping.

And then there were the tabloids. Apparently making a shit-ton of money made him a celebrity. He appeared at clubs in LA with starlets and singers on his arm. There are still a few articles here and there wondering what happened to him.

"They don't know where you went. Or why you stopped making appearances."

"If I fire you, you could make decent money selling a story to them."

"That would violate the terms of my nondisclosure agreement with the agency."

His voice is mocking. "And that would be

unethical."

I nod my head yes, realizing that somehow I've gotten backed against the wall.

There was only one recent article, a small piece in a local Maine newspaper stating that Rhys and Emily Rochester passed away on their yacht when they were caught by a storm. It doesn't go into details about the accident, which seems strange. Don't newspapers love gory details? Maybe they were staying quiet out of respect for the family. Or maybe they somehow couldn't get details the way they did for other families. Maybe Beau hushed it up.

They're survived by their daughter, Paige Rochester. Her guardian, Beau Rochester, a favorite of venture capitalists in California, declined to comment.

He's in front of me, only inches away. Heat from his body seeps into mine. We're standing in a wood-floor hallway in Maine. I have no sweater, no socks. I should be freezing, but instead I'm burning up. Like there's fire inside him, and it's making me warm.

I look up at him, searching, searching. For what?

"Your eyes," he mutters, sounding almost angry about it.

"What about them?"

"They're alight. I could drown in them."

"Like the man in the song?"

He leans on the wall, hand by my head. His other hand traces my arm, the curve of a forearm, the dimple of my elbow. The goose bumps rising on my shoulder. I lift my chin as if to shrink away from his touch. No, as if to give him access. And he takes it. The backs of his knuckles run over my chest. It's a strange place, those few inches. Not overtly sexual, but neither are they someplace a man like him should ever touch.

It awakens me. I feel like what he said I was—alight. His thumb moves to the hollow at the base of my throat, and I suck in a breath. "You shouldn't be—you shouldn't—"

"I shouldn't touch you," he murmurs.

"You're my boss."

"And you're the nanny."

His thumb continues its rhythm. "Why don't you stop?"

"I told you, sweetheart. Life is unethical."

He's looking at my lips in the dark hallway, and I lick them. His body turns tense against mine. I can feel the way his muscles harden. There's maybe an inch between us, but we're connected by invisible strings. I can feel every line of tension, every point of wanting.

His head descends, a dark shadow.

"Tell me to stop," he mutters against my lips.

It's already a kiss, those words. I close my eyes. A tear leaks down the side of my cheek. It's not sadness. It's more than that. It's desire. It's feeling anything at all after being numb for so long. I'm more afraid of this than a free fall down the cliff. "Don't stop."

"Fuck," he says, wrapping his hand around my throat. Choking me, but without the pressure. It doesn't hurt, but it makes me feel strange, as if I'm being possessed. "You're too innocent for the things I want to do to you."

"What do you want to do to me?"

"Everything."

There's fear. Of course there is. He can make me feel things.

I don't know if I can ever close Pandora's box again after this. What does *everything* even include? He's too much for me in every way, but I still want a taste.

I want to open the lid and peek inside.

"One thing," I whisper. "You can do one thing to me."

It's surrender and a request at the same time. I want this much from him, this slice in time.

We're not in his room. Not in mine. I can pretend this hallway is neutral territory. That this won't change anything. He presses his lips against mine. They're warmer than I thought they'd be. Softer. He lets me get used to him there for a moment before pulling back. And then again. I've been kissed a few times. It feels like the mashing of lips. It feels like being plundered. This is entirely different. He brushes his lips against mine again, this time from a different angle. A million nerve endings become alight. I let out a shuddery breath.

His hand moves from my neck to my jaw. He tilts my head back so I'm open to him. He looks down at me with a dark expression I take as a warning.

There's only a narrow window of world. My eyelids feel low. It's a trance-like state, a dreamy place where my body is liquid and he's hard as rock.

He brushes the backs of his knuckles across my clavicle. And down my arm. It occurs to me how naked I am compared to a regular day. My nightgown isn't revealing. It's a plain gray cotton. Nothing sexy, but he looks at me as if he's enraptured.

My nipples are hard points against the thin

fabric.

He traces the curve of my breast, not touching where I need it most. It can't be an accident. He can see them standing stiff and sensitive for him. Instead he circles around and around. It's maddening. It's cruel. "You're a bastard," I whisper.

He laughs softly. "Only one thing," he murmurs. "We already kissed."

"Two things." It comes out on an embarrassing moan.

He rewards me with a hard pinch on my nipple, and I let out a small, muffled shriek. "Ah, ah, Ms. Mendoza. You can't make noise. No matter how much it hurts."

It would be so easy to move farther down the hall. To move into one of our bedrooms. We could even go downstairs and never be heard up on the second floor, but that would make this more real. In the dream, where I'm still warm from hearing him sing that old sea shanty, I have to be quiet. "Do it again," I breathe out, more movement than sound.

He does it again, pinching hard enough that I gasp. He doesn't let go, either. The pain turns numb, but I'm held taut, my whole body a string between his fingers, knowing that the moment he lets go, it will feel like fire.

It's with a casual tap of his thumb, a small gesture that speaks to familiarity. That's how he lets go of me, and I whimper in near-silence as the pain registers.

"Like this?" he asks.

And I shake my head—no, no, no. I don't want him to stop, but it hurts to keep going. There lies the problem with our relationship. With my entire life.

"No?" he asks, his touch turning gentle again. He slides his hand down to my hip and pulls me close. I can feel his erection against my belly, a hard, hot length that proves how much he's enjoying this. That turns me on even more than his touch could. This is a man who knows beauty. Who's been with more women than I'll ever meet. He could have anyone. He wants me. "What if I felt between those pretty legs of yours? Would you be wet?"

"I don't know," I lie.

He gives me a small smile. "Let's find out. Pull up your nightgown."

Oh God. It would be so much easier if he lifted the fabric himself. I would let him do anything to me. It's different to participate. To be the engine of my own destruction.

I grasp the hem in trembling hands and lift.

He takes a half step back to examine me, and I almost chicken out. I almost drop the nightgown and run down the hall into my room. Like some scared little virgin. That's probably what he expects me to do. He even lifts an eyebrow, waiting and watching.

When I don't move he gives me a thorough perusal.

"Pink," he murmurs.

And I don't know what he means until I remember dressing after my shower.

Grabbing the worn pair of pink panties that have been washed a hundred times. There's probably something humiliating like a hole somewhere. I never thought anyone would see them. I never thought *he* would see them.

"Pull them down," he says.

I close my eyes. Can I do this? "Three things," I murmur, more to myself.

The air in the hallway should be freezing, but I don't feel the cold. There's only heat in his gaze across my skin. I push the waistband of my panties down to my thighs.

"Good girl," he murmurs.

The words wash over me in a rush of pleasure and embarrassment. I know it's wrong to be doing this with my boss, with a man so much older than me, with a man who has power over me—but it feels sharper because of those things. Sweeter because of them, too.

He leans close, enough that I can feel the warmth of the words against my temple. "Spread your legs. And hold your nightgown higher."

It's hard to spread them with my panties around my thighs. I can only open them about a foot apart. The confinement of the elastic makes it hotter.

As if I'm tied up for him in a net of my own making.

Even my hands are restricted. I'm holding up the fabric, which means I can't do anything else. I can't pull him closer. I can't push him away. As long as I follow his commands, I'm trapped against this wall, open for whatever he wants.

He traces designs over my rib cage, and I shrink away from the ticklish sensation. He draws a heart on my stomach, and I suck in a breath. There's letters written into my skin along the side of my hip, but I can't make out the words.

I'm on fire. He's teasing me, the same way he teased my breasts. Avoiding the place where I need him most. Pride has no space in this hallway. I push my hips forward, trying to tempt him.

Needing him more than my dignity.

Finally he pushes two fingers between my legs.

He's nimble and light when he wants to be. Precise when it comes to pain. But he's a blunt force in my pussy, two fingers rubbing hard and fast, making me pull up on my toes.

I realize that he wants me this way. Off-balance.

When I move my hips in a rhythm against his hand, he pulls back.

The wall is trembling at my back. No, I'm the one trembling. "Please, please, please."

"You beg so pretty. Men would die to have you, you know that?"

That makes me laugh, an unsteady, breathy sound. "I'm no one."

"You are softer and more vulnerable than anything I've ever seen. It's like touching water."

There's something not quite right about that. He shouldn't want me vulnerable. Or maybe I shouldn't like him being such a fortress. The thought flits through my head. Then his lips touch mine, and it's gone.

He takes it deeper this time, using his tongue to dampen my lips, biting me gently, teasing me so I lean forward. His large palm covers my breast, and I moan into his mouth.

There's a glaring absence of his hand between my legs. I'm still holding up my nightgown. My panties are still wrapped tight around each thigh, but he doesn't touch me.

When he kisses me again, I bite down on his lower lip.

"I'm still waiting for the third thing," I say, and I know I'm pouting. It feels almost flirty. A little seductive. Who is this woman? Maybe I am someone men would die to have, right now.

He shakes in silent laughter, but it doesn't matter. It doesn't matter when his hand slides down my stomach to my sex. He pushes two fingers into the wetness and squeezes them together around my clit. I catch a high-pitched noise in my throat.

His dark gaze meets mine. We both know I have to be quiet.

We both know that I can't.

Mr. Rochester presses his palm over my mouth. The moan that follows is muffled. He begins a slow and steady pace, fucking me with his fingers, rubbing the heel of his hand against my clit. I gasp and moan into his other hand. My hips rock to meet him, to make the friction harder, but whenever I do that he pulls back. He demands that I follow his rhythm, his pressure.

He demands that I follow him in every way, and I close my eyes, yielding to him.

He rewards that with a firmer grip. It's possession, the way he holds me between my legs. I feel owned by him. Other men might die to have me, but he already does.

My mouth is captured by his hand, so he can't kiss me. Not there. But he does kiss me on the forehead, on the tip of my nose. Innocent places that are made filthy by the way his hand fucks me without mercy. A kiss beneath his hand, right on my chin. And then one at the hollow of my neck. He puts his tongue against my pulse and licks.

I won't survive him. It's too much, too hard, too fast.

Too much feeling after a lifetime of trying to be numb.

I bite his fingers, and it's like he was waiting for that. As if it's the switch that turns him on, that small amount of pain. He fucks me proper, then. Hard enough that I'm caught up in the current. There's no more thinking, no more doubt. Only the endless rapids that carry me on and on and on. Farther than I knew existed. And then there's the cliff at the end. I go over the edge of the water, clenching my thighs around his hand, biting down on the flesh of his palm, holding tight to him as if he can save me from coming apart.

He pulls back when I flinch, but he keeps rocking his hand against me with soft pulses, carrying me through the final eddies of climax until I'm lax against the wall.

For long moments there's only the mingled sounds of our breathing, the scent of sex in the air. It's thick with the knowledge that he's still hard. Will he ask me to join him in his bedroom?

What will my answer be?

Strange that I don't know.

He pulls my panties up with a too-kind gentleness. I don't like this side of him. I don't trust it. I open my hands, and my nightgown covers me. We are decent again, except for the glisten of my arousal on his fingertips.

"Tell me about that boy you have back home. The one who's always texting you."

I stiffen against the wall. "Why do you care so much about Noah?"

His lips curve. "Well, you just confirmed that he texts you."

It is a night for secrets. "He's like a brother to me."

"So he doesn't do this?" Mr. Rochester asks, brushing his lips against mine. He brings his palm up to my hip. "He doesn't hold you like this?"

"No," I whisper.

"Does he know? Does he know he'll never have you?"

"I don't know." I don't know how to tell him. He's never made an overt advance, but I've seen the way he looks at me sometimes. Maybe it's just my imagination. That's what I keep hoping.

"You should tell him." The words come out on a sigh. I breathe him in, and he breathes me back. "It's better to cut him loose, better that he doesn't keep hoping."

"Are you speaking from experience?"

He rests his forehead against mine. He's large and strong, but in this moment it feels like I'm holding him together. "There are worse things than never having the woman you want."

"Like what?"

"Go to sleep, Ms. Mendoza."

There are worse things than never having the woman you want. Having her? Finding out she isn't who you thought she was? *Losing her?* The secrets have reached the end of their tether. It is a fire that's burned out, leaving only ice in its wake.

There will be no invitation to his room. I feel both disappointment and relief.

"Good night, Mr. Rochester."

CHAPTER TEN
BEAU ROCHESTER

I RETURN TO my room smelling of sex.

Jane's arousal dampens my fingertips.

I'm hard as iron beneath flannel. There's no way I'm going to sleep like this. Instead I hit the shower in my room, turning the water hot. Cold water would be one option. The restrained option. The stop-lusting-after-your-nanny option. Instead I turn the knob all the way to the right. Water burns my shoulders and my chest. It runs in rivulets down my abs, down my legs.

I grasp my cock in a tight fist, eyes closed, imagining Jane's dark eyes. Her sweet pussy. Her slender legs, revealed in that hallway.

She should have been afraid of me. I held her slender neck in my hand. God, she should have run away from me. Called the agency and told them what I did. Sued me for sexual harassment. Instead she lifted that pointed little chin and asked me to touch her.

One thing, she said. *You can do one thing to me.*

The list of things I want to do to her lithe body is long and inventive, but if I can only do one thing then I wanted to kiss her. Simple. Innocent, even. Though there was nothing innocent about the way I claimed her mouth or the way she responded to me.

Two things. I touched her sweet breasts. Teardrop shaped, those breasts. Sloping into a wide curve. Nipples a little darker than I expected. Darker than her lips. She loved when I pinched them. I think my nanny likes it a little bit rough.

I'm still waiting for the third thing, she said, her voice pure sex. I reached into those velvet folds, inside that slick channel. I fucked her with my fingers, and now, in the shower, I use the same hand to fuck myself. I pretend it's her sweet pussy that I'm rutting against. One arm leans against the cool tile. The other jacks my cock. I close my eyes and rock my hips, pretending I'd lifted her in that hallway. I could have fucked her. She would have let me. Her bare pussy would feel so warm and wet. It would be a heaven I don't deserve.

Climax builds from the base of my spine. It runs through my body like electricity, heating me more than the steaming water. I grunt through the final thrusts, my breath catching.

"Jane, Jane, Jane." It's a chant and a prayer.

Orgasm rips through my body, and I come in hard, uneven jerks, spilling white liquid across white tile. It slips into the water stream and swirls down the drain.

I'm panting.

"What the fuck are you doing?" I mutter to myself.

Nothing good.

That young woman has an entire future ahead of her. That has nothing to do with a broke down billionaire who's practically living like a hermit. Would still be living like a hermit if it weren't for Paige. She's the only reason I'm moderately civilized these days.

That's really an overstatement of the situation. I'm mostly feral.

I blow out a breath and towel off outside the shower.

When I lay back in bed, I pick up my phone. It's glowing from some text messages. Mateo. My oldest friend. We'd been chatting on and off all day. I scan his last texts, something about a new Netflix original series he's being considered to do.

Sorry, I text back. *Parenting duty called.*

It's 3 in the morning. Doesn't she have a bedtime?

Bad dream. She's been having them. Dreams where her mother and father are still alive. Where they're still in danger. Where they're out on a boat, unable to get back to shore.

Which means a sea shanty probably wasn't the best song to sing.

It was the only one I knew. The Rochesters weren't a loving family, even at the best of times. There were no lullabies, only the hauling of lobster and the shouting of bills unpaid. I know better than to complain. Other people had it worse. People like Jane had it worse.

An orphan, the same as Paige. But different. At least Paige has family. She has me.

A sad excuse for family, but I'll do my best.

Can I help? Mateo texts this, and I run a hand over my face. We're both clueless bachelors who have no business raising a child, but it's been good to have someone to bounce ideas off of. It was his idea to contact the Bassett Agency. They source a lot of nannies for the famous actors and celebrities he knows in LA.

We're okay, I think. The nanny started working. How's that going?

I just finger fucked her in the hallway. I just jerked off in the shower while dreaming about fucking her. That's how it's going, but I'm not going to text any of that to my good friend. He would bust my balls, as he should. That's not why I'm keeping it secret, though.

It feels private, what happened between me and her.

Which is the scariest part of all.

Fine, I say instead. *Paige seems to like her.*

That's true enough. I watched them from the window of my study while they explored outside the house and painted rocks. They're lining the old antique sidebars and tables downstairs, those rocks. It would probably make Emily Rochester turn over in her grave to see them on her expensive furniture.

I doubt Paige had that kind of freedom before.

There isn't much I can give her. Love. Affection.

Those things are foreign to me.

Money is all I have to offer, and the nanny is what I've purchased.

Don't scare her away, Mateo texts back.

That's the problem with having old friends. He knows what I'm capable of. *I don't need to play nice*, I type. *That's what the money's for.*

He sends me back a middle finger, but he knows I'm right. That's the way the world works.

Rich bastards like me get to order a pretty woman to spread her thighs. If she had a family, if she had a support system, maybe she would have said no.

The ache in my chest is protectiveness. I hate it.

I made her orgasm, but that doesn't make it right.

Don't touch her again, Rochester.

That's what I tell myself, but even as I drift off to sleep I see the count in my head. One, two, three things I can do to her. What if she asks for a fourth thing? A fifth? She invades my dreams the same way she does every night since she arrived, except now I know how she feels when she comes, her clit slippery, her body shuddering against mine.

CHAPTER ELEVEN

JANE MENDOZA

PAIGE IS HER usual chatty self during breakfast.

She doesn't seem affected by the nightmare, which is a relief to me. I'm extremely distracted by what happened after. Why did I let him touch me? Why did I want him to touch me?

After stuffing ourselves with waffles and syrup and butter, we put on our hoodies and socks and shoes and head outside. There's other warm clothing for her—mittens and scarves and hats, but I'm determined to do only what is possible and not stress over what's not.

We have something of a routine by now.

I pick up her set of paints and brushes. She grabs a square-bottomed basket we found in a large shed out back. By the time we return, it will be filled with painted rocks, fallen branches, interesting leaves and the occasional snail shell.

This time when we reach a selection of

smooth, wide rocks, I have a plan.

We set up on a dry patch of grass, the rocks arrayed around us. Out come the paint brushes and selection of colors. Normally we do swirls and stars and hearts. Occasionally we dive into the more ambitious designs—such as painting the kitten. Kitten comes with us, stalking through the forest like a grown-up on the hunt while we work.

I pick up a fine-tipped brush and draw on a dark rock with white paint. *1 + 6 =*

Without saying a word, I pass the wet rock to her.

She becomes very still, staring at what I've done. Children are smart. Smarter than most adults think. I learned that in foster homes, when social workers and foster parents would speak to us like we couldn't see what was in front of our eyes. It's not about adding up numbers, though she's that kind of smart, too. It's about understanding what I'm doing and why. About knowing that I'm trying to help her, even if she's fighting me tooth and nail. About doing the hardest possible thing instead of lying on the ground in pain.

She lets out a breath.

The same way it's happened for other children who've experienced trauma at a young age, school has become the no-fly zone. It's become the enemy territory.

Another shaky breath. Then she draws a shaky seven in cerulean blue.

I'm almost afraid to move, afraid to break the spell.

She draws the seven with that line through the middle. Where does that line come from? I'm not sure, but that's not how I draw my sevens. I wonder if it was her mother or father who taught her how to write it like that.

I remember enough about the caterpillar worksheet to write all of them on stones. It's embedded into my mind. I'll probably turn eighty and still remember clearly that time Mr. Rochester said, *And here on this worksheet, you add up these numbers and put the answer in the caterpillar's asshole. They've got a real garden theme going on here, don't they?*

I pick up another stone and write another equation. *9 + 9 =*

She doesn't stop to think about it this time. Her small hand writes the number *18*.

Words dance on my tongue. *That's amazing. You're doing it. Thank you so much. I know this was hard for you, but you're strong and smart and so brave.*

Also, *would it be possible for you to write this on paper?*

I keep my lips pressed together as we make it through the whole worksheet using rocks instead of paper and paint instead of a neatly sharpened number 2 pencil. When we're finished I pass over a blank stone, and she immediately begins doodling her designs.

Pulling out my cheap phone, I snap photos of each of the equations.

Some shift in the light makes me look up. A shadow stands at the window of his study. His office looks down on where we spend our time.

Does he see what's written on the rocks? Does he even care?

Fuck her education, he said, but I don't think he meant it.

Right there, outside, using the Wi-Fi beaming from the house, because Lord knows there's no signal up here on the cliff, I email the photos to the teacher with a note. I explain that due to her grief, this is the way she can express herself, and if they are concerned with concept understanding, she's proven that in this form.

Now I understand how mama bears feel. I would fight off hunters for her. I didn't even birth her from my body. I've only known her for six weeks, but I feel protective of her.

That evening after dinner I call Noah.

"This is a surprise," he says above the sounds of a pot clattering. I can imagine him standing at the rusted cream-colored stove in his apartment, his roommates playing something on the Xbox in the living room. "Usually I'm the one calling you. And getting your voicemail."

"I'm sorry." Guilt churns my stomach. "I've been wrapped up in this job. There's not really a clear boundary between work and personal time."

That is the truth. I just finished doing the dishes and in a few minutes I have to help Paige with her bath time and then put her to bed. It's rather like being someone's actual mother. I suppose that's why I do feel so close to her. And why the person doing this job needs to live here.

It's the truth, but not the whole truth. That's why I still feel guilty. The truth is I never quite know what to say to Noah. I love him like a brother, and I don't want to disappoint him, but it feels like that's inevitable. We want different things.

Movement and voices on the other end. Then the sound of a door shutting.

And quiet.

"I'm in my room," he says. "The guys pooled

their money for a game that just came out, and they've been playing nonstop. I went to my shift and came back, and they were still there. I don't think they moved for ten hours."

I give a snort-laugh.

That sounds like his roommates. One of them is as broke as Noah, working hard to pay the bills. The other two are going to college on their parents' dime. Splitting the cheap rent in the old two-bedroom apartment instead of the more expensive dorm rooms is how they're helping out.

It's a totally different kind of existence.

"Did Ryan at least stop locking you out of your room?" Ryan is a total manwhore. One day after Noah ignored the tie on the doorknob to go in and grab his work badge, Ryan started locking the door whenever he had sex. Which was a lot.

"We have a truce."

"How'd you manage that?"

"Told him if he did it again, I'd stab pins through his condoms."

"You wouldn't!"

"I totally would. And he knew it. That's the only reason why he stopped. I was sick and tired of sleeping on the sofa while they played their games." There are some shifting sounds, and I imagine him lounging on his bed. I've been in that room plenty of times—the door open, of course. Him on one side of the bed, me on the other, trying to throw Skittles into his mouth. "That's one benefit of your job. No roommate drama."

I look around my small room. I haven't made much of a personal dent here. There's a glass of water on the nightstand. A black charger cable waits for me to plug in. My clothes are neatly packed away in the dresser, the luggage—still muddy from its one use—is stowed in the closet. You can't really see that it's my room, but it feels like mine.

He's touched me, he's kissed me.

My room is one boundary that Mr. Rochester has not crossed.

"I don't miss the drama." My roomies were good people, but we were packed in three to a room. It was tight but the rent was dirt cheap. Doesn't matter how hard you try to get along. When there's less than two hundred square feet per person, you're gonna have problems. "Or the claustrophobia. This place is pretty massive."

"Rich people need some place to keep all the shit they buy."

The acid in his tone makes me flinch. "I don't know why you hate rich people so much. I mean, it sucks being poor, but they didn't make us this way."

"The whole capitalist system relies on some people doing menial labor for shit wages."

I sigh. "I don't want to argue with you, and maybe you're right, but I just can't hate these people for being born rich. Or working hard and earning money. That's the dream, right?"

"It's not *your* dream. Or are they rubbing off on you?"

"No," I say, feeling defensive. "I still want to go to college and become a social worker, so I can help people. That's my dream, but I need money to do it."

"I would have helped you." There's hurt in his voice. He's offered that a few times, but there's just no way I can accept his money. We have so little of it. We work so hard for it, and there's never quite enough to pay all the bills.

"And I appreciate that. It means more than you can know, but I couldn't. I just couldn't. That's your money for you to go to college, and fulfill your own dreams."

He snorts. "Such as?"

That makes me smile. "I don't know. There was that time you filled Mr. Lawson's car with frozen hot dogs. That could be your true calling."

"Hey, those were cooked from the sun by the time he found out. That's like free food."

I laugh softly. "I don't know what you want to be when you grow up."

"Hell, Jane. I feel like I'm a hundred years old sometimes."

"We've lived through a lot."

He falls silent, and I know he's thinking about the past—same as me. We came from nothing. Less than nothing. We're the rejects in society, the kids that no one wanted. It leaves a mark on a person that never goes away. I'm grateful that no matter how much Paige is struggling right now, she'll never have that experience. She has a home here.

Tears prick my eyes, but I force a fake smile in the dimly lit room where he can't see me. "What about becoming a doctor? You could help people heal from diseases."

"And pander to the pharmaceutical gods, handing out pills like candy? No, thank you."

"Then you can be a lawyer. Defend the innocent."

"They're all fucking guilty of something."

I give an exasperated laugh. There's like a fifty percent chance he's only saying this to mess with me. "No wonder you feel a hundred years old.

You're so cynical."

"Hey, just because I'm paranoid doesn't mean they're not out to get me."

"Maybe become a social worker with me. We know how the system works, how kids get left behind. We can make it so that doesn't happen anymore."

"I could never do that," he says quietly.

"Why not?"

"Because the first dad I met who beat his kids, I'd punch him in the gut so many times he'd die. And then I'd end up in jail. I'm too pretty for that, Jane."

I suck in a breath, because he's right. There's true evil in this world. He knows it. I know it. Even if I get a degree and become a social worker, I won't be able to right every wrong.

That's a pipe dream, and he's kind for pretending it might really work.

"There must be some dream you have," I say. "Something you imagine when it's dark, and you're about to fall asleep, and Ryan is staying over at someone else's place."

"Yeah," he says softly. "There's a dream."

"Well?"

"It's you, Jane. You're the dream I have in those moments, when I'm too sleepy to stop myself."

A fist closes around my throat. Heat floods my eyes. I've always suspected, always *known,* if I'm honest, that he wanted more from me than I could give him, but he's never come out and said it. I've never had to tell him no before. "Noah."

"It's okay. I know you don't think about me that way. And I know you're made for better things."

"No, Noah. It's not like that. We're the same, you and I—"

"We're not. You're going places in your life. Hell, you've already gone somewhere. And me? I'm going to be here, working at the same grocery store for the rest of my life. They'll promote me to assistant manager someday, and that will be it for me."

"Don't."

"Don't what? Don't tell the truth? Go back to your rich people. That's where you belong."

There's a click. I look at my screen. *Call ended.*

CHAPTER TWELVE

JANE MENDOZA

M Y EYES ARE puffy from crying the next day, but I scrub them hard with soap and paste a pretend smile on my face. I have an email back from the school agreeing to accept the work with stones and paint in lieu of scanned pages. There's lots of verbiage about all the exceptions being made, and how grateful we should be, but the important thing is that it's going to work.

Paige is going to pass first grade, and she's going to do it herself.

My pride knows no bounds, and we forage together through the woods, painting onto rocks and trees and even a particularly large mushroom. We recreate worksheets about writing and math and social studies. When we're done with eight of them, we move on to creative designs—the abstract swirls and splashes she loves so much.

We take a break at a patch of wild blueberries, pulling them off sharp branches until our hands are pink and our lips are colored blue.

A text comes in on my phone. I tense, thinking it might be Noah. Instead it's an unknown number. *Meet me in my study tonight at 9 p.m.*

Mr. Rochester, then.

I wonder if he already knows about the school thing. I'm excited to tell him.

Groggy and heartbroken, but also excited.

While wandering, we come across a tree that has a large wound in it.

"Hit by lightning," Paige says, her small voice knowledgeable.

We take out our paints, and she goes to work on the ten-inch canvas made by lightning while I relax with my back against another tree. Twenty minutes later she steps back, and there's a woman in her painting with blonde hair and a sunny smile.

My throat feels tight. "Your mom?"

A quick nod.

"She would be so proud of you. The way you're handling schoolwork right now."

"You think so? Uncle Beau was mad at me for not doing it."

"You *are* doing it now. It counts just as much on rocks as it does on paper."

She gives me a small, unexpected grin before

scampering away through the forest.

Paige goes to sleep at eight, so I have a full hour after I put her down to wait. I only make it for thirty minutes before I head to his study. No matter how much he claims not to care about her education, he does care.

No matter how grumpy he pretends to be, he'll be happy about this.

I knock on the door to his study at eight thirty-six p.m.

"Enter."

I bound into the study, full of energy and hope for the future. And stop abruptly when I see his expression. His eyes are full of mystery and menace. His lips are pressed to a flat line. Even now, even looking angry, he looks handsome.

It's a cruel world. Unethical, as he would say, to make someone so mean look so beautiful.

"What's wrong?" I ask.

"Sit down."

I'm too full of energy to sit down. "Paige has made the most exciting progress. She's doing her schoolwork. She's doing it outside on rocks, with paint, but that doesn't matter. It still counts. I already heard back from the teacher and—"

"I saw that. Excellent work. I must say, I didn't expect that from you."

The way he says *from you* makes me stiffen. As if there's something wrong with me. "I thought you'd be pleased about this. You said she had to pass first grade. Now she will."

"Sit down, please."

The word please makes me frown. He still sounds angry, but at least I can sit down and find out why. "Did something happen?"

"I suppose you could say that. I got a report back from a private security firm. Turns out the background check that Bassett Agency did was not quite comprehensive."

I frown. "I don't have any… felonies or anything."

"No." A faint smile. "No misdemeanors. Not even a single detention at school."

"Why do you sound like that's a bad thing?"

"It's not, of course. Every good uncle wishes that his niece is raised by such a paragon in society."

I narrow my eyes and say nothing. This is not a good talk.

"Your packet from Bassett Agency didn't include your medical records." He shifts through some pages on his desk. They look long. Like physically long pieces of paper. Medical charts? He runs his hand over something that looks like an X-ray. "Lots of broken bones."

My blood runs cold. "How did you get that? There's a privacy law for health records."

"Money talks, sweetheart."

I swallow, thinking back to Noah's words about doctors being slaves to the pharmaceutical companies. Did the hospitals sell me out for a few dollars?

Go back to your rich people, Noah said. *That's where you belong.*

But I don't belong here.

"Why are you doing this?" I ask, my voice hoarse.

"You're spending more time with Paige than any other person. I'd like to know who you are. More than just some platitudes written in a recommendation letter."

"I spend more time with her because *you* ignore her."

"I know everything that happens in her life."

Emboldened by my outrage, I roll my eyes. "You don't spend time with her. You don't talk to her. You don't even eat dinner with her, which would be so easy."

"So easy," he says, as if testing the words. "I've never had any experience with children. Never wanted any experience with them. Being made a legal guardian of a child doesn't magically turn you into a good parent."

"You think I don't know that? I came from the foster care system. It's full of terrible, terrible legal guardians, people who never should have been put in charge of a child."

"People like me," he says, his voice challenging.

"Would you rather she go to a house that can't afford heat, a place where the dogs get more to eat than the humans, a family that beats you for crying for your parents?"

"That's what it was like for you?" His voice is hard.

"You care about Paige. I know you do."

A soft smile. "I don't care about anyone but myself."

I lift my chin. "Then why aren't you still in Los Angeles partying every night?"

"God," he says. "You think it's because I'm selfless? I didn't leave that scene for Paige. I left a year before that even happened, because I was sick to death of all the silicone and the cocaine and the fucking nameless women."

"They had names," I say, my teeth clenched together. "Whether you knew them or not."

"I know your name." Four simple words that

should not be provocative, but they are.

"You know more than that. Everything about me, really. Things you have no right to know."

"Like Noah Palmer."

"You already knew about him before. He wrote me a reference."

"The cheese counter. Yes, I remember. You didn't mention you were fucking him. I'm not sure you should be getting a recommendation letter from a boyfriend."

"We aren't dating. And we aren't f—" I choke on the word. "We aren't fucking."

"He couldn't make you come?" he asks blandly.

"We never—" I glare at him. "Not that it's any of your business, but we've never had sex."

"There's a report from your foster mother that said you two were close. She thought you were fucking on the regular. Put you on birth control to make sure there were no babies."

My nostrils flare. "My last foster mother was crazy and borderline abusive. I put up with her to graduate high school, and then I got out of there."

"Yeah." He picks up a piece of paper and frowns. "She comments on that. Apparently you weren't very grateful for all the work she did."

"She did *nothing*. She fostered kids for the

monthly check, and I took care of the little ones."

"Sounds like a real bitch," he says, his tone casual.

"I didn't say that."

"I don't mind saying it. Would you like me to have her pulled from the foster system? Those kids can stay with other terrible legal guardians, instead."

I let out a coarse laugh. "You can do that, right? Because you're rich. Because you built a billion-dollar company before you turned thirty, so now you can rule the world, right?"

"Basically. Yes. That sounds about right. It's nice."

"The whole capitalist system relies on some people doing menial labor for shit wages," I say, throwing Noah's words at Mr. Rochester. "You're only rich because some people are poor."

He raises an eyebrow. "And you're only mad about it because you're one of the poor people."

I stand up. I'm shaking, furious. I need this job but I can't keep it. Not like this. "I may be a poor person, but I'm a *person*. I deserve respect. You don't get to dig around in my medical records and in my personal life like you have a right to it."

My feet move me toward the door before I

even know what I'm doing. I'm leaving, and he's following me. Then he's standing there, his palm against the heavy wood, his expression fierce.

"I'm a bastard," he breathes, and I close my eyes in reluctant surrender.

"I know."

"She broke your wrist, didn't she?" He picks up my hand. The palm has mostly healed from the tree. There are red streaks like lines through marble. On the outside of my wrist there's a half-moon scar where the bone once poked through skin. "The bitch?"

"Yes," I whisper.

"I already have the kids being moved out of her house. And I have an investigation started on the worker who placed you there and said nothing when you broke three bones under her care."

"Why are you angry at me?"

"I'm not. I'm angry at the whole fucking world, Jane. You're just close to me."

"That's not—"

A sympathetic smile. "Fair?"

I swallow. "I'm glad you got the kids out."

"Don't thank me. Fight me." He shoves me up against the door, and I make a soft sound of surprise. "Hit me. Beat me. Mark me. Break my bones, one for every one you broke."

"No," I say, shaking my head back and forth against the wood. It's so thick I can feel the striations in the wood as I move. "I won't."

"I'd do it, you know that, right? I'd break my own bones. I'd fight a goddamn dragon if it means I could go back and undo that hurt you felt."

A wild laugh bursts out of me. Or maybe it's a sob, because I do know that about him. He's such a bastard to me, but I also see the good in him. The way he cares about me, even though he doesn't want to. "I know."

He presses his lips against mine, artless and heavy. "Go on."

And I do—I bite him, I bite at his lips, not hard enough to draw blood, but hard enough to hurt him. He doesn't flinch away. He takes my rage and my pain inside himself, and becomes what I need in this moment. My hands turn into fists and I bang them against his chest. He's strong enough to take it. I'm the endless, frantic sea, and he's the cliffside, stoic and strong.

He gentles, and I subside with a soft cry. It turns into a real kiss then, something loving. I let out a shaky breath, and he breathes it in. He takes everything I have to give—the anger and the hurt, but also the fear. I've lived with so much of it, and he doesn't turn away.

CHAPTER THIRTEEN
BEAU ROCHESTER

I GREW UP with a healthy respect for the sea. It was tinged with fear. We all knew men who had gone out to fish and never come home. Every family had lost people, but we did not shrink from the waves. Instead we learned the proper way to ride them.

One weekend when I was out with my father, a storm came in quick.

It had been drilled to us early—never turn your back on the ocean. But the ocean was everywhere on this day. It came up on the sides in heavy waves. It knocked our boat around like it was a plastic toy. Rain came down so thick it felt like a curtain.

My brother went over the side. A wave came three yards above the bow. Rope caught him around his boot. A slippery deck did the rest.

I screamed for my dad, but he was fighting with the flooded engine. I threw out the life buoy.

It danced around in the wild waves, like a bright kite that I had to maneuver.

Rhys couldn't catch it. He kept reaching, but then his hand didn't come back up. Or his head. The waves tossed him again, and I could barely see his shadow in the storm.

I jumped in after him. Darkness and chaos. Water in my lungs.

I woke up six weeks later in the hospital. It became a local legend, the way I snapped my brother out of the jaws of death. I didn't even get hurt, aside from the pneumonia that I caught after. Plenty of girls in high school were ready to visit the back of my truck based on my reputation. Rhys never forgave me for being the hero of that story.

The feeling in the water, of knowing that I'm being tossed and turned by a force much more powerful than myself, being unable to see, to breathe, to think—that's what it felt like to get custody of Paige. Darkness and chaos. Water in my lungs.

Somewhere in hell Rhys probably doesn't forgive me for being here, either.

Here in my study—his study—with a beautiful woman.

"Harder," I tell her, and she listens to me like

a good girl, biting at my lips, pounding at my chest with her tiny fists. It's like being attacked by a hummingbird.

"Why am I doing this?" she asks, breathless.

"Because you're angry, and I'm the one close to you."

"I'm not—I can't be angry."

She can't be angry because there's not enough space in her life for that.

There's only survival.

The world has a lot to answer for. Reading her file made me angry. Looking at the hospital records made me nauseous. Actually talking to her social worker on the phone made me want to burn everything down. She was raised like a feral cat behind the barn.

I should leave her alone. Send her back to that boy in Houston. Let them get married and have babies. They would live near the poverty line, the two of them, but they'd love their kids. They would be the kind of parents Paige never had.

I should leave her alone, but I won't. I want her too bad.

"I can't stop thinking about your pussy," I murmur.

Her eyes go wide. "I thought we could pretend that didn't happen."

What did she think was going to happen? That I was going to feel her swollen, slick pussy and not come back for more? "You can pretend. Pretend to be surprised when I touch you, pretend to be shocked when you come."

There's a delicate flush climbing her neck. I touch it with a lazy forefinger, tracing designs into the pink skin. Beautiful, I spell out at the base of her throat.

She swallows hard. "Shouldn't we—? I think we should be professional."

"Think some more," I tell her, leaning close for a kiss.

She tastes as sweet as I remember from that night, like honey and milk and salt. All things nourishment. I drink from her lips, taking my time.

There's no rush. Not like LA. Not like before. We have the rest of eternity, and I use it to brush my lips against hers. To suck her bottom lip between mine. To bite down gently.

To explore every inch of her, to map out her expressions.

"You taste so good," I murmur between bites. "But I want something else with that mouth."

Such a doe, this one. Eyes wide. "I've never—"

"You've never given a blowjob before?"

That's a surprise. I would have thought she'd tried that with her cheese counter boy. Or at least with someone else in high school. She's absolutely gorgeous. A knockout. With that thick mane of black hair and dark eyes, those long lashes and full lips, to look at her is to get hard. How did she evade every horny boy? It's almost enough to make me think twice. I should let her go back to that boring, wholesome life of hers, but God, that mouth.

"I'll teach you. Get on your knees."

She stands very still and very tall. There's a gentle sway, but no breeze in the room. I'm pushing every one of her boundaries tonight. This is a test. She drops suddenly, one knee to the floor, then the other. Her lips are trembling. It shouldn't be so sexy, the way she shakes. This is her own personal ocean. Darkness and chaos. Water in her lungs.

I put my thumb to her lips. "Open for me."

She does, and I push inside. For a moment I only enjoy the heat, the wetness.

My cock is like steel in my slacks, wanting to be where my thumb is. I push deeper, feeling the warmth of her tongue.

She struggles, not knowing what to do, coming to terms with the invasion.

She looks up at me with trust. She may not know that's what it is, but I know, and it scares the living hell out of me.

"Suck," I tell her gently, and she closes her lips around me.

The suction is sweet. I enjoy that for a few moments, along with the faint wet sounds. Is there anything hotter than silence with only those faint wet sounds? It means I'm going down on a woman or she's going down on me.

Then I begin to move my thumb in and out of her mouth, a little forward, a little back. And then again. It's more than fucking her. It's teaching her.

Showing her the rhythm my cock will use.

I push my thumb farther back, mostly because I want to see her gag. I want to see what happens when she's pushed beyond her limit. It's beautiful. And so wrong of me. I'm not a good man. She should not be kneeling in my office, but I'm not going to make her leave. Tears form at the corners of her eyes and dance a path down her cheeks.

"I made you come," I murmur, my thumb still on her tongue. "I made you feel good that night. Do you want to make me feel good, too?"

She nods, and the sweet sincerity in her eyes almost unmans me. What a delicious little morsel.

How she escaped Houston with this much innocence astounds me. It's not that she hasn't seen darkness, because I know she has. Her records are proof of that.

It's that it hasn't touched her, marked her, changed her.

Part of me is relieved that I might not change her, either. That she will escape this house unscathed by my secrets. But part of me wants to mark her.

I pull my thumb out and tap it against her lips. "My cock will be bigger than this. Are you ready? I want you to say, Yes, Mr. Rochester."

Her lips move against my thumb in a kiss as she forms the words. "Yes, Mr. Rochester."

I open my pants. My cock springs out, heavy and thick for her. She lets out this adorable little gasp. No wonder men like virgins. I can't remember ever admiring a lack of experience. I thought it would be better if a woman knew how to take me deep, if she knew how to work her tongue, but seeing Jane's eyes wide makes me ten feet tall.

I fist myself and stroke a couple times. I'm giving her time to get used to the idea. That's what I tell myself, but in reality I'm giving her time to run away.

She's far too innocent for what I want to do to her. Even if she acts tough, even if she looks seductive as hell on her knees, she's soft inside.

My hand speeds up. Maybe I can just come on her face. Maybe that will somehow defile her less than making her suck me. Except she leans forward. A swipe of her tongue across my cock makes me suck in a breath. "Jesus."

She does it again, and my hips buck toward her.

"Is this right?" she asks, and fuck me, her tone is pure feminine wisdom. She may not be experienced, but she knows exactly what she's doing to me.

Any impulse I have to protect her, any hope that I can get out of this unscathed evaporates. I stroke her hair and praise her as she learns what makes me groan. "You're so beautiful. So sweet. So good. Don't stop, sweetheart. I'm dying here. I'm dying for you."

Then I lose the ability to speak. She looks up at me with those dark doe eyes. The climax rises out of the base of my spine. It spreads through my entire body like an electric shock. I stifle a yell as I hold on to her hair, tight, too tight, needing the connection to her as I come.

I'm panting, out of breath as she releases my

cock.

Need heats her dark brown eyes, making them molten. Someone needs to come. There's a million ways I could make her come. With my fingers. With my mouth. In a few minutes to recover, with my cock. All of those feel too intimate at the moment. Too emotional. I'm already exposed. I fist her hair and make her look at me. She pleads with a soft whimper.

I shove my shoe between her knees. "Ride it."

There's a moment of shock. Indecision. She wonders if I'm pushing her too far. I wonder the same damn thing. And then she lowers herself onto my shoe. I'm wearing old black oxfords, the leather worn and cracked. Her pussy rubs against it, slick and sensitive. Reaction flares in her expression. Her desire soaks into the fabric laces. She's too hesitant, so I nudge her with my knee. It's just enough humiliation to make her cheeks heat and her hips buck.

"Please," she mumbles.

I tighten my grip in her hair and guide her, faster and faster, harder and harder, until her eyes squeeze shut and tears leak down her cheeks and a sharp cry escapes her as she comes.

CHAPTER FOURTEEN
JANE MENDOZA

THERE'S A WOMAN who looks like Paige all grown up.

She's wearing a soft blue dress, long sleeves and long skirt that flares at the bottom into a white fabric with tiny red flowers. Her hair is down, curls moving in the breeze. The cliff rises to meet her. The sun beams down on her. The entire Maine coast seems to embrace this woman, but I'm watching from behind cold panes of glass. There's no light in the house. Only darkness.

I open my eyes and stare at the silent room.

Something compels me out of bed. A sound? Did Paige have another nightmare? It might have woken me up, though I don't remember hearing anything.

The woman. The woman in my dream.

That must have been what Paige's mother looked like.

I'm drawn to the window, as if searching for

the long-ago image of her standing on the cliff. The moon hangs in the sky. I expect the cliff to be empty at this time of night, but there's a shadow of movement. A woman in a dress walks through the trees. Not a woman, a child.

It's Paige.

She's wearing her nightgown, the one I put her to bed with four hours ago. It's actually a pale blue color with white stripes and little red flowers on it.

The fourth room down. That's Mr. Rochester's room. I knock and then without waiting open the door. He sits up in bed, the hard planes of his chest and shoulders glinting in the moonlight, his dark hair tousled.

"What?" he barks.

"It's Paige." I'm breathless. "I saw her walking outside."

Before he gets out of bed, I'm down the steps in a flurry of cold. I swing a jacket on and slide into my sneakers as I step outside. A freezing wind slams into me, almost propelling me back in the house. I force my way past it and break into a run.

The trees form an arrow in a cluster, pointing toward the house. That's where I saw her enter the forest. She's gone now. I look around wildly for a flash of that pale blue nightgown or a streak of dirty blonde hair. Nothing.

"Paige!" Hands grab me from behind, and I shriek.

"It's me." A low voice. Mr. Rochester. "Which way did she go?"

"I don't know." There's a puff of air where my warm breath turns cold. "I saw her walking this way through the trees. But she's not here anymore. Where could she go?"

He looks out over the ocean. Over the cliff. It seems impossible that she could have jumped, but it's so slippery and treacherous at night. You can't see where you put your feet. There's fog in the air tonight, making the stones extra slippery. What if she fell?

We have the same fear. He and I, we move toward the cliff at the same time. We could look over the edge, but we would not see a kitten with nine lives who managed to land on her feet. She would be hurt and crying—or worse.

I reach the very edge, where the rock already begins to slope. It's been worn away, this corner—by wind and rain. By sleet. It's already pointing down.

You have to get this far out to see over. I hold my breath and peek. Nothing. Only darkness. Relief washes through me. It takes me a full thirty seconds to sweep my gaze over the full length of it, part of it steep and vertical, part of it a long slope.

No sign of her.

A huge gust of wind hits me from behind, and I let out a little moan at the cold and shock. It blows into my nightgown, freezing wetness against my skin. I hold myself rigid against the force, but it makes me take a step forward.

That's when my foot hits something wet. A patch on the rock—mud, probably. My body moves in an uncontrolled slide, a sharp scream entering the air.

It's me. I'm the one screaming as I head directly for the edge.

Pain in my shoulder. A large hand clamps down on me and pulls me back. I grasp onto it, onto him, and hold on tight. We both slide down. He grabs my wrist in a punishing grip. There's a hard yank that feels like it pops my arm from the socket—and then I'm sprawled onto the hard, wet rock. There's an uneasy absence of sound above the roar of the ocean. Nothing. No one. I'm alone up here. I scramble over to the edge and down.

On part of the slope about ten feet down, Mr. Rochester is sprawled. He used his momentum, surging forward to push me back onto solid ground.

"Beau," I scream.

He doesn't move.

"Oh my God. Oh my God." I don't know how to get to him without falling the same way he did. And even if I get down there, how will I lift him back up? "Hold on, just hold on."

"You called me Beau," he says, his voice strained.

"Oh thank God you're alive." My heart is beating out of my chest. "I thought you died."

He gives an uneven laugh. "It would probably feel better than this."

"I'm coming down there!"

"Don't you dare. I'll fucking throttle you. Go find Paige, and get her back inside."

I bite my lip, uncertain. Maybe I should find Paige. She's small and defenseless. At least Beau seems conscious right now. And relatively stable. Despite the slope, he's probably not going to roll down like it's a grassy hill. Except what if he has internal bleeding? He might be delirious. He might be dying. "No, I'm not leaving you here. Paige is probably off somewhere painting a rock she found. Or maybe she even got back into bed."

He swears extensively. I'm pretty sure I hear some words that have to do with boats and sailing and fish mixed in there, the old Maine vernacular running true. He puts a hand to his head. "I think I'm all in one piece. Mostly. I need a large glass of whiskey. Or a bottle."

"First we need to get you out of there. Do you think we need to call in like… a rescue team?" I'm envisioning something with ropes and pulleys and a stretcher. "I'll call nine-one-one."

"Absolutely not. The last thing I need is the boys I went to high school with cutting me open. They couldn't even dissect a fucking frog in biology."

"I feel like they give them training for stuff like this."

"No. I can climb up."

"You can climb up? What are you, Spider-man?"

"I did some rock climbing out at Big Sur. It was more dangerous than this."

"The fact that you just fell and almost died seems to contradict what you're saying."

"I didn't die or even come close to it. I'm mildly winded."

"Then why are you just lying there."

"I'm resting. It's restful here. Next time I go camping, fuck White Mountain. I'm just gonna roll out a tent right here and look up at the stars."

You can't see a single star because of the fog. "I'm going to call nine-one-one."

"Don't." He forces himself to a sitting position. "I'm coming."

"You're at least ten feet away from me."

"Fifteen, but the angle of the rock is almost forty-five degrees. This wouldn't even count as rock climbing. It's advanced hiking, and I could do it hammered."

"You might be bleeding internally."

He stands, looking unsteady as hell. I hope he was right about doing this drunk, because that's what he looks like right now. He grasps onto a ridge above him and pulls. The first part of the way works pretty well, because like he said, it's not that steep.

But the drop right where I'm standing is a solid five feet.

There's a grunt. "I might need your help with this last part."

"Listen. For the record I vote calling for help. If we both go over the edge and die in the sea, I want it to be clear that I was against this."

"Fine," he says between gritted teeth. "Don't help."

I make sure my feet are planted on fairly dry ground, grasp his hand, and pull as hard as I can.

There's a moment of uncertainty where we waver, his weight more than my strength, but then we collapse on the rock. It's hard and cold and pointy in some places—but it's never felt so good as right now. I press my cheek against it and let out a sob of relief.

Can adrenaline make you drunk? I feel a little hammered as I stand up. I stagger a little, but he doesn't move from the ground. "Beau? Mr. Rochester?"

"I like it when you call me Beau," he says without moving.

"Can you walk?"

"I may have understated how much pain I was in down there."

"Oh my God, you are bleeding internally."

"I'm not." I can hear the scowl in his voice, though he doesn't lift his head. "It's my damned leg. I don't think I can make it back to the house without a walking stick."

"I'm not getting you a walking stick. Your leg is broken."

"Well, I can crawl there. It will be undignified as fuck, but I probably deserve it."

"You need crutches. And a cast. And X-rays. And a hospital, goddamn it."

"The same way you had a hospital when you

broke your wrist? Twice?"

"Yes," I say, thoroughly aggravated at him. "That's why you were able to bribe people to get the hospital records. Which I'm still mad about."

"Thirty-six years climbing over these rocks, hauling lobsters on a boat, some truly crazy illegal stunts while high as a kite in Los Angeles, and I've somehow managed to never break a bone." He glances at me. "You're dangerous, Jane Mendoza."

"And you're delirious."

"Find Paige."

"Fine, but you had better be here when I get back or I'm going to throttle you."

It takes me about fifteen minutes that feels like fifteen hours before I find her curled up in a pile of pine needles, the kitten tucked under her chin. The painting we did of her mother only a few feet away, and I know without asking that it's what drew her out tonight.

I wake her gently and let her know that Mr. Rochester's been hurt. She figures out on her own that he was hurt while looking for her, so I hold her close and dry her tears. "It wasn't your fault that he fell, but you need to stop going out at night. If you get scared or lonely or sad, you come to me. Even if you need to go outside, I'll come with you. Promise?"

"Promise," she says in a wavery voice.

We hold up Mr. Rochester on either side and limp together into the house. The kitten trails behind. It's a slow and painful journey but it feels like we're a small family.

CHAPTER FIFTEEN
JANE MENDOZA

H E DIDN'T JUST break one bone. He broke three and fractured another. The hospital sends him in for surgery while I wait at home with Paige, glued to my cell phone.

It's enough to earn him doctor-ordered bed rest.

Even a crutch could aggravate the healing process.

He was only gone from the house for a total of twelve hours, but everything changes. If an ordinary grumpy asshole Mr. Rochester was a storm, then the new bed-ridden Mr. Rochester is an entire hurricane.

"I want that whiskey," he growls from the bed.

I continue picking up dirty clothes that are strewn across the floor without meeting his gaze. "You can't have whiskey with the pain medicine."

"Fuck the pain medicine. I'm not going to

take it. I want whiskey."

"Why on earth wouldn't you take pain medicine?"

A low growl. "If you don't give it to me, I'm going downstairs myself."

"Do you just want me to feel guilty?" I say, throwing up my hands. Tears prick my eyes. I hate being emotional at a time like this. I can't seem to stop.

"Guilty? Why would you feel guilty?"

"I know what happened out there. You pushed me back onto the ground and let yourself fall instead. The only reason you have three broken bones is because of me."

"God save me from crying females. It's not your fault. It's not Paige's fault. It's not anybody's fault but this damn cliff and the ocean and a thousand years of history."

"I'm going to stand here crying until you take the pain meds." It's not hard to make that threat, because I'm already standing here crying. When I was sixteen I talked back to my foster mother. She held my wrist so hard and twisted that it fractured. I didn't cry the whole time she did it. I didn't cry that night when I went to bed or in the morning when the school nurse realized what happened and sent me to the hospital. Now I'm a watering pot. It doesn't make any sense.

"Christ." He takes the two pills sitting on the nightstand and swallows them dry.

A hard sniffle is my attempt to stop crying. "I could drink the whiskey for you."

"Get out."

He continues to be a terrible patient, arguing every time he needs medicine, growling because he's clearly in pain, demanding whiskey along with brandy and finally tequila.

Mrs. Fairfax bustles in to clean his room and the rest of the house. She leaves promptly at noon, the same way she does every day. "I don't take care of invalids," she says on her way out the door. "Don't get paid to do that."

CHAPTER SIXTEEN
BEAU ROCHESTER

GOD SAVE ME from crying females.

Jane with her gorgeous wide doe eyes. I can't believe how close she came to going over the side of that cliff. My body is made of salt and water, made to beat against these Maine rocks. She's fragile. Slender. Young. The fall could have killed her.

My mind supplies that image for me. Every time I close my eyes, it's not my own fall that I see. It's hers. She could have gone over the cliff— and then what?

It would have broken me to see her hurt, or worse, killed.

I've gone far too deep with this girl. The sex was wrong. Inappropriate. Definitely taboo to ever touch the nanny, but it was only supposed to be sex. An approximation of sex. Touching and kissing. Fucking her mouth. Does that count as sex?

Now I'm feeling things for her I have no business feeling.

And she's clearly feeling them, too.

I know what happened out there. You pushed me back onto the ground and let yourself fall instead. The only reason you have three broken bones is because of me.

What was I supposed to do? Let her fall?

She stood in my room, so proud and so strong. She's made of twigs, really. Twigs and leaves and whatever weight fills the air. She's delicate—but she made me take my pain medicine. I hate feeling groggy. I hate losing control. And I'm losing control to Jane.

I'm alone in the room now, but for how long?

She'll be back, taking care of me, nursing me back to health, and I'll fucking fall in love with her. It's a disaster. I need to fix this—for my sake and for hers. She's nineteen with dreams of her own. She doesn't need to be saddled with a bastard like me and my millions of secrets.

The world already looks a little more hazy from the meds.

At least my leg throbs less.

I pick up my phone. Mateo. That's who I should call. My old friend would give me shit about falling off a cliff, but he'd help me.

Probably.

Unless he's shooting some commercial.

Instead I scroll to the bottom and dial Zoey Aldridge.

She makes me wait ten rings before answering. I can imagine her in her black-lacquer apartment, nails clicking against a glass tabletop while she watches her iPhone ring.

"Hello, Beau." There's that sultry voice I remember.

"Zoey."

"Didn't think I'd be hearing from you again. After I got your parting gift. In the mail."

She's pissed. Of course she'd be pissed. I didn't feel like meeting her just to break up, so I sent her something pretty from Tiffany's. Not like she returned it.

In the silence that follows I can hear her calculating her next move. It's sweet, actually. Being with someone I can understand. Not like Jane with her dark eyes and mystery.

"I broke my leg. In three places."

"Is that your way of saying you miss me?"

"It's my way of inviting you to Maine."

"If you want me to fuck you with your leg broken, you can think again."

"I did miss this," I say with a laugh. It's the

same way you miss the rough open seas. Not because they were pleasant, but because it's all you knew. "Pick out a present. Send me the link. And get on a fucking plane."

"You're a bastard, Beau Rochester. Everyone told me."

"Everyone was right." Zoey Aldridge is a beautiful woman, but I don't want to fuck her. I can't imagine ever doing it again. The terrifying part is that I can't imagine ever wanting any woman who isn't Jane again. That's untenable. It won't do. That is why I need Zoey here, a wedge between us. I need to push Jane away, because I'm already too close.

CHAPTER SEVENTEEN
JANE MENDOZA

T URNS OUT THAT Paige's private school has a counselor on staff, so we schedule a Zoom call. The counselor sends a note beforehand that Mr. Rochester should plan to attend. When I mention it to him, he growls a threatening and creative use of swear words.

The first counseling session ends up being helpful for both her guilt over Mr. Rochester getting hurt and her reluctance to do schoolwork. The woman asks gentle questions about why she feels safer holding a paintbrush than a pencil, without judgment. We make an appointment for her to meet with Paige online once a week so they can work through some of this together.

I'm heating up the dinner that Mrs. Fairfax left when the doorbell rings.

A woman stands on the step, a man in a suit holding an umbrella over her head. She looks only vaguely familiar in a blonde-and-beautiful kind of way.

I'm sure we've never met.

A limo waits behind them. I stare at them, struck for a moment between the differences in our arrivals. Me, in an economy Toyota Prius with Walmart luggage in the freezing rain. Her, with a chauffeured driver, her no-doubt Louis Vuitton bags in the trunk.

"I'm here for Beau," she says with a kind, sympathetic smile.

"Like a doctor?"

She scrunches her nose, as if embarrassed for me. "We're together."

Oh. Oh. I've been here for three months now, and I've never seen him go on a date. That doesn't mean he's not with someone. He could have a long-distance relationship. Hell, he could have gone to New Hampshire to see her late at night, and I wouldn't have known about it.

"Right. Let me just…" It seems weird to let a stranger into the house when we aren't expecting her. I mean technically she could be a thief. Though I don't know why a thief would have a Tory Burch trench coat. Seems unlikely you'd hire a limo for a theft. "Let me check with Beau."

And I proceed to close the door in her face.

"What's going on?" Paige asks as I walk by the

kitchen.

"Nothing, sweetheart. Be there in a minute." I head up the stairs, feeling like an idiot times a hundred. I'm muttering to myself—excuses, denials. Reasons why I closed the door on someone who is most likely a treasured guest. "There's a child in the house. You can't be too careful."

I open Beau's bedroom door to find him typing away on his laptop.

"We said no work," I say, standing there like an outsider. In so many ways, an outsider. Why did I ever think we were like a family? What kind of insane adrenaline rush made that thought run through my head. Mr. Rochester, and I will call him Mr. Rochester from now on, is my boss.

"You said no work," he says without looking up. "I can type just as good sitting down as standing up. The hydrocodone makes it so I can tell people to get their heads out of their asses."

"You don't do that already?"

"I can say it better now."

"There's someone at the door."

He does look up then. "Who?"

We live on a remote cliffside. It's not exactly flush with visitors. Mrs. Fairfax comes once a day. She brings any groceries or supplies we need. The

Uber driver was right about that—the only place that winding, terrifying road leads is the Coach House.

"A woman. Umm, I probably should have asked for her name. She said you're dating."

His eyes become veiled. "I'm not dating anyone."

"So I should send her away?"

"What does she look like?"

"You're going to date a random crazy person if they look good?"

A quirk of his lips. "I'm trying to figure out who she is. Not gauge if I should date her."

"Pretty. Blonde. Rich."

He sighs. "Shockingly that does help me figure it out. It's Zoey. Send her up."

"Mr. Rochester—"

"What happened to calling me Beau?"

"I guess that stopped when you started dating some pretty rich blonde woman."

An eyebrow rises. "Are you jealous?"

"No," I say. "I need to call Noah anyway and let him know what happened."

Mr. Rochester narrows his eyes. "Send up Zoey. And then leave us alone. I think she can handle my needs from here on out."

I slam the door, which is childish. I'm feeling

childish at the moment. I let Zoey in with a brittle smile and go back to heating up the lobster casserole. Sure enough, Zoey comes down to get servings of the dinner for both of them. They eat together in his room.

Only a few days ago, he kissed me. He touched me. He made me come.

What was I thinking?

Besides the fact that he was very good at it.

I'm no one to him. My cheeks heat with embarrassment. I was convenient to him. He probably imagined her beautiful blonde hair when I went down on him in the study.

When I finally make it to my bedroom, I don't call Noah.

We've exchanged a few texts since our big fight, but nothing too personal. Mostly memes we think the other person will like. He would probably be upset if I told him about last night. He'd probably think that was a good reason to come home. After how dumb I feel about getting intimate with Mr. Rochester, I might even agree, but I won't leave Paige right now.

Instead, in the dark, curled up in the comforter, I google Beau Rochester and Zoey.

The search results make my stomach clench.

They appear at movie premieres and popular

nightclubs. There's a photo of them standing in a group with some famous actors I recognize. They all have huge grins on their beautiful faces. What did he say out in the cold? That he had committed "some truly crazy illegal stunts while high as a kite in Los Angeles." This group seems like they'd be down for whatever.

God, I'm a fool.

Did you think you'd hook up with the playboy Beau Rochester and get your picture in the tabloids? He asked me that once. I didn't even know what he was talking about then.

The tabloids speculate if his breakup with Zoey Aldridge is the reason he left the social scene—heartbroken and unable to bear seeing her around. Little do they know that they're still together. I wonder if the tabloids would be interested in printing that they're holed up in a bedroom in a Maine mansion right now.

If I fire you, you could make decent money selling a story to them.

Now I understand why some people make unethical choices. We don't set out to become that person. It's bitterness that hardens us. I won't sell information about Beau Rochester, but I can understand the desire to for revenge in the face of my humiliation.

According to Wikipedia, Zoey Aldridge got her big break on this reality dating show years ago. Since then she's been linked to multiple musicians and Silicon Valley billionaires. She has her own jewelry and perfume lines in major department stores.

And then there's me. Orphan. Poor. Nanny.

I had the audacity to think that Beau Rochester was interested in me for anything more than a quick fuck up against the door in his study.

The next day I wake up in a slow simmering state of frustration. Even Mrs. Fairfax senses my mood, because she makes my favorite breakfast—blueberry pancakes.

We're eating when Zoey breezes into the kitchen wearing a loose silk top and skinny jeans. "We're having a little dinner party the day after tomorrow. Beau needs some cheering up. He's been locked away here in the middle of nowhere for months. No wonder he broke his leg."

"He fell off the cliff," Paige informs her soberly.

That earns her a winning smile from Zoey. "Would you like to attend a beautiful dinner party with all of Uncle Beau's friends?"

She glances at me, unsure of her answer.

I give her an encouraging nod, but Zoey isn't

waiting for an answer.

"We'll need to discuss the menu," she says to Mrs. Fairfax. I wait for a comment about how Mrs. Fairfax isn't paid to do that, but apparently no one says no to Zoey. "Flowers will be delivered. Guests will stay at the Lighthouse Inn in Portsmouth; I've already made arrangements for them." Her gaze falls on me. "And you can be available to take Paige to bed when she's tired. Our parties can go all night long."

CHAPTER EIGHTEEN
JANE MENDOZA

THE FEELING OF frustration continues through the next day, where only Zoey goes in and out of Mr. Rochester's room. I haven't even seen him in forty-eight hours, and it feels strange after living in the same house for months.

As I'm coming out of Paige's room, I see Zoey stepping down from the attic. Wait. Why is that place forbidden for me but she can go there? It seems like if anyone needs access to Paige's old childhood things, it would be the nanny. I'm tired of Beau's secrets. I'm tired of being locked out, after he made me feel like I finally belonged.

When she goes into his bedroom, I approach the attic stairs.

Part of me still wants to pull back, to follow Mr. Rochester's orders, to be the good girl. That's what I've always tried to be. Look where it's gotten me. Nowhere.

I open the door and climb the steps. I'm not

even sure what I'm supposed to find up here. What is so secretive that Mr. Rochester forbade me to go up here?

And why was Zoey here? Does Mr. Rochester know that she's exploring his house?

Did you think you'd hook up with the playboy Beau Rochester and get your picture in the tabloids? Precious little of that here in Eben Cape.

I'm suspicious of Zoey, even though that's ridiculous. She clearly has her own money; she doesn't need his. And I have no right to be protective of him.

Not when he's pushing me away.

The attic looks about the way I remember it, more sundrenched now than before, light coming in through grimy dormers. I see the same fine china and Legos. The same paintings and rowboat. Nothing that would make Mr. Rochester forbid me from coming up here.

Something in the box catches my attention.

A little book that's blue and velvet. Not a book. A journal. There's handwriting scrawled across the lines—large, loopy, definitely feminine handwriting. I should put this back in the box. Or show it to Beau. Let him decide what to do with it.

Instead I find myself opening to the first page.

The wedding was yesterday. B didn't come. I shouldn't be surprised, but I am.

Is this the private journal of Paige's mother? Is B Beau Rochester? It seems likely after what I heard yesterday. I should definitely not be reading this, but I can't seem to stop. I flip a few pages. A few months pass. She does not write every day.

R got an invitation to the charity dinner next month. I will have to sit next to the mayor's wife and smile and pretend like I don't know she fucked my husband.

My cheeks heat. I toss the diary back into the box. I shouldn't be reading that. Whether it's written by Paige's mother or not, it's clearly very private.

No wonder Mr. Rochester didn't want me looking up here.

I wonder if he's read the diary. I wonder if he's the *B* who didn't attend her wedding. It takes an embarrassingly high amount of discipline to close the diary and set it back down in the box. Then I go back downstairs. I have no idea what Zoey was doing up here. Nothing good. That's what my gut tells me.

I wander downstairs, but I'm too restless to sit down, even though Paige is engrossed in an animated movie I've watched with her a thousand times already.

The kitchen is usually tidy to the point of being sterile. Mrs. Fairfax is very good about cleaning as she works. There's usually only one pot on the stove at any given time. Everything ends up wrapped neatly in the fridge.

It's like a bomb went off in the kitchen right now. A food bomb. There's chopped vegetables in an unruly pile and meat resting on a slab and water boiling over on the stove.

"Mrs. Fairfax!"

She turns and grabs the plastic handles with her bare hands. Boiling water sloshes over her skin. She screeches, and I run over to her, guiding her hands beneath a stream of cold water from the tap. "It's too much," she mutters to herself. "I can't do it. I should quit."

"Shhh," I say, making soothing sounds. Maybe it would help me to have Zoey's dinner party become a disaster, but it wouldn't help Paige if we lost our cook. The only things I know how to make are Pop-Tarts and boxed mac and cheese. "I'll help you. I can't cook, but I can cut things up and follow directions. I'm yours to order around."

She looks suspicious.

"Seriously." I wave in the direction of the

vegetables, where a pile of zucchini rests. "Are these next? Do you want them sliced or cubed or what?"

"Fine," she says with a reluctant sigh. "And thank you, I suppose."

She shows me how she wants them chopped, and I get to work. As she moves things onto the stove and into the oven, the kitchen begins to look more orderly. When she doesn't have something for me to prepare, I wipe down the counters and keep things clean.

"This smells amazing," I say, using pot holders to take something out of the oven. I don't even know what it is, but it makes my stomach grumble.

"Don't know why these rich folks need so much food."

I offer a companionable shrug. "I wouldn't know."

She gives me a dark, knowing look. "Maybe if you become Mrs. Rochester, you'll find out."

My cheeks burn. Does she know what Beau and I have done together? She must be guessing. She wasn't in that hallway with us at night. She wasn't in his office when I went down on him. Except she looks at me like she does know. Maybe I'm see-through. I'm giving it away. "That's never going to happen. I'm not stupid."

Well, perhaps I was stupid for a while. I didn't think he'd marry me. I just didn't think about anything at all. I let myself feel things without thinking about the consequences.

And now there's Zoey in the house. She's the consequence.

"Never gonna happen," she agrees. "Not for that other one, either. The pretty one."

"Zoey," I say, my voice grim.

"That's her. Zoey. He's not going to marry her either."

"Why not?"

"Because he's a bad man. And bad men are better off alone."

Despite the fact that I've been frustrated at him, outrage rises. "He's not a bad man. And no one deserves to be alone."

"He's got lots of money," she says, her voice contemplative. "Plenty of women who'd marry him just for that, but they'd live to regret it, they would."

"We shouldn't talk about our boss that way," I say, my voice stiff.

Her smile turns sly. "That what you call him? Your boss?"

"I'm only Paige's nanny. That's all." *Liar,*

whispers a voice in my head. *You want to be more.*

"I see the way you look at him," she says, heaving a large platter into the oven. "And more importantly, I see the way he looks at you."

"How does he look at me?"

"Like he's going to eat you up. Eat the meat off your bones and spit the rest of you out."

"That's a terrible analogy. I'm not fish."

She shrugs. "It's your own life you're risking."

"My life?" Does she mean I'm going to ruin it by falling for some guy who's inappropriate for me? Or does she mean actual risk, which is how it sounded? "I think you're exaggerating."

"You heard about what happened to that other Mrs. Rochester, didn't you?"

"She died in a boating accident."

"Some that says that. Others that say she was murdered. Her husband, you know. Beau's brother. They were always fools, both of them. Violent. Mean."

I shiver in the warm kitchen. "The newspaper said it was an accident."

She keeps going as if I never spoke. "And some says her spirit never really left. Her ghost roams the cliffs looking for Beau to save her from her husband."

Unease clenches my stomach. "That's not

real."

Cool brown eyes meet mine over a steaming pot. "I wouldn't go into the attic again, Ms. Mendoza. You go looking for ghosts, you just might find them."

CHAPTER NINETEEN
Jane Mendoza

I'M NOT SURE I've ever really attended anything called a dinner party. My father went to work and came home. On a good night we'd watch a baking show together. There wasn't a large group of family and friends, which is why I went into the state's custody when he had a heart attack.

My foster homes could barely put food on the table, much less invite people over.

Apparently a dinner party involves a lot more than good food. A party rental company arrives in the afternoon, dropping off fine china, wineglasses, cutlery, a table runner, and iridescent sashes to go across the wooden dining room chairs.

A truck from a local vineyard arrives with bottles of wine and hard cider. A separate delivery from a liquor store arrives with cases full of every other kind of alcohol.

Then a package arrives through UPS next-day air that requires a signature. Turns out there's a cake from a famous bakery in New York City inside. I didn't even know you could get these kinds of things delivered.

Paige frets about the dinner party, about what to wear, about meeting all of Uncle Beau's friends. "What if they don't like me?" she asks me.

"They will love you. You're kind and adorable and smart. Of course they'll love you."

She frowns. "Of course you say that. You're paid to like me."

I sit up straighter in the armchair. We're sitting in one of the living areas, a Monopoly board open between us, way more pieces of property and stacks of cash on her side than mine. "Hey. I like you for yourself. Not because I'm paid to do it."

"But I gave you so much trouble with the schoolwork."

I circle the coffee table and sit next to her on the leather couch. "You are a brilliant little girl, and it's an honor to get to see you every day. I'm not mad one second about the schoolwork. You had a hard time, and you pushed through. That's something to be proud about."

"I don't want to go to the dinner party."

I look away, not sure how to handle this. "Well, I guess we could talk to Mr. Rochester about it and see what he thinks. But I feel like if you're invited, you should go. It could be fun."

"Mama had dinner parties."

My heart sinks. "She did?"

"Big ones like this. With fancy food. I never liked the fancy food."

Mrs. Fairfax works past noon today on dishes full of paella with king prawns, chicken, and mussels. There's also a hanger steak with greens and a saffron risotto. In other words, I've never eaten most of what's being served tonight. "We can find something to snack on before the dinner starts. That way you're not hungry."

"Why can't you come and sit next to me?"

Because I wasn't invited. Because I'm the help. I don't know how best to explain this to Paige. Noah would probably have something snarky to say about class systems, but I just feel lower than dirt right now. "I'm sorry, honey. I wish I could."

It's not entirely true. I don't want to sit and watch Zoey Aldridge fawn over Mr. Rochester. Or worse, watch Mr. Rochester fawn over her. Though I am curious about the food and the decor. I'm curious what it would feel like to be rich.

"If you're not allowed to go, then I'm not going to go."

I have to grin at her impassioned response. "You're loyal, and that's a good thing. I appreciate it, but you belong there. You belong right there with your uncle Beau. Just think, he might need your help getting something and not want to look weak in front of his friends. You could help him out."

She considers this. "I did like looking at the cake. It's so tall!"

"So it's settled," I say. "You're going."

"I'm gonna wear my Electric Company shirt," she says in a warning tone. The shirt is very soft from being washed so many times. The yellow ink threatens to fall off.

"That sounds like a great idea. Very festive."

I'm determined to keep a smile on my face throughout the evening. It should really be like any other evening where I work taking care of Paige. This is my job. I was a fool for ever thinking of it like anything else. It's only a small, sad amount of vanity that has me changing my clothes in late afternoon. Of course I don't put on anything fancy. I don't even own anything fancy. I'm windswept from walking outside, so I put on a fresh black T-shirt and jeans, wash my face, and brush my hair into a ponytail. It does not make me look like Zoey Aldridge in the least.

The doorbell rings for the first time at six thirty. And it continues to ring until there are eight new people in the house. Luckily the table is long enough to hold everyone.

I walk Paige downstairs right before dinner starts. She's vibrating with nerves and excitement. People stand around in one of the formal sitting areas, a fire burning. Zoey holds court in a gorgeous black dress and high heels. Mr. Rochester sits in an armchair, facing away from us.

Paige squeezes my hand, and I give her a gentle squeeze back.

"See?" I whisper. "There's Uncle Beau."

A few of the people standing with glasses of wine look our way. I feel a flush heat my cheeks. I don't want to be noticed by them. Maybe it's immature of me, but I want to push Paige into Mr. Rochester's arms and then run away. Instead I stand there because she needs me. Even if I end up looking like a forlorn fool in front of these rich people.

I crouch down to meet her eyes. "What's wrong, honey?"

Her eyes are wide as saucers. She doesn't answer. I think she's frozen in fear.

Mr. Rochester turns to face us.

"Paige," he says, and it seems to break the ice.

She runs to him and buries her face in his arm. She still looks shy with the group, but at least she's found her anchor.

I give him a grateful smile and then step into the hallway.

"Wait," he says.

Run, my mind supplies, but instead I freeze. A deer in the headlights. Nothing good will happen to me inside that room. The command in his voice holds me in place. I'm out of sight right now, and I stand very still, hoping he'll think I've already left.

"Jane."

I'm Jane, now. The way he became Beau. It's a boundary that we don't need to cross.

I take a step back to the doorway, hoping that he needs me to fetch something. An innocuous errand for me to run. Anything but what I suspect will happen next. "Yes, Mr. Rochester?"

His full name reminds him of his place. And mine.

He quirks his lips. "Come join us."

"Oh no. I couldn't possibly."

"Why not? I'm sure my friends want to meet the woman I've been spending so much time with."

It's like a bomb goes off in the room. Not the

explosive kind. The magnetic kind that shuts down electricity in an entire city. The casual movements stop. The murmurs between people go silent. A few eyebrows rise. Zoey Aldridge wears a frozen gorgeous smile.

I don't even know what my face is doing, but it can't be good. How could he just come out and basically imply that we're having sex in a room full of people I don't know?

"You're allowed to come now," Paige says, full of excitement about this new development.

Which somehow makes it worse.

"I don't know," I stammer. "I'm not dressed for a party."

"It's just a casual affair," Mr. Rochester says. "You don't mind, do you?"

He addresses the question to the group, but he looks right at Zoey. She manages a graceful demur. "I'm not sure she'd be comfortable with us. We're a rowdy group when we get together."

"She can handle it," he says.

Paige comes to grab my two fingers and drag me into the room. I did want to experience this party, to feel what it's like to be rich, but not like this. Not as the help. Not while I'm being paraded as Beau Rochester's convenient sex partner.

"What are you doing?" I whisper at him while Paige wanders over to the bar cart, examining the colorful liquids, the amber and burgundy, the rarer aqua blue and chartreuse.

"You need to eat dinner. Why not eat with us?"

"I would rather starve."

"Are we that evil?"

"No. Not because of that. Because I'm this charity case now."

"You're not a charity case. You have more reason to be here than any of the other people. They're only here to get a look at me so they can gossip later."

I give him a sideways glance. "If that's true, why did you invite them?"

"I didn't. Zoey did."

That makes me roll my eyes. "It's your house."

"Maybe I was curious to see what you'd make of them."

"Well, they're paying more per night at the Lighthouse Inn than I have in my bank account."

"You need money for something?"

"Spoken like a rich person. I need money for everything."

A soft chuckle. "Fair enough. Spend the evening with us. Spend it with me. It's going to be a major chore for you, I'm sure. Much worse than changing diapers and wiping hands."

"Why does everyone think six-year-olds still wear diapers?"

"The food should be good, at least."

Before I can reply two handsome men appear. They look like brothers.

Specifically, they could easily pass for the Hemsworth brothers, one of them taller and leaner, the other one muscled and smiling. Both of them blond and blue-eyed.

One has his arm slung over the other one in a casual embrace. It's like a meme where you have to guess whether they're dating or siblings.

"Don't let this ugly bastard monopolize your time," the taller one says. "We want to talk with you. We're always eager to meet new people."

"You smell fresh blood," Mr. Rochester says in a dry tone.

"She'll come back in one piece," says the older one.

His hair's slightly longer. You have to look carefully to catalog the difference between them. He takes my arm and leads me away from Mr. Rochester.

My heart thumps against my rib cage. I'm so

far out of my depth, it's ridiculous.

We end up standing next to the fireplace. One of them procures a glass of wine. I take a sip just so I have something to do. And wince at the sharp acidity. Somehow I always thought expensive wine would taste better than what I once tried at Olive Garden. Apparently not.

"Tell us everything," the younger one says.

"But especially the parts that Beau would hate for you to say."

That makes me laugh. These two are definitely out for fresh blood, but there's something charming about it. Not that I'm going to spill any deep dark secrets. "There's nothing to tell, really. I work for him. I help Paige with schoolwork, get her dressed, that kind of thing."

"The nanny," one says.

"The au pair," from the other one. "What's the difference between a nanny and an au pair?"

"I'm not sure," I say honestly. "The agency that hired me placed both of them. I think technically I'm a live-in nanny, but I'm not that worried about my job title."

"So you do live here. I wondered about that."

I nod and take a sip. The wine burns all the way down. I can't believe how much they spent per case of this. Does it hurt everyone like this?

It's like instant heartburn in a bottle.

"Does Beau wander around in only his boxers?" The younger one looks hungry for that piece of information, which makes me wonder again if they're gay and together. Or brothers.

"What did you say your name was?"

They exchange an amused glance. "Where the hell did he find you?" one of them says.

"Oh," I say, clutching the wine stem. "Am I supposed to already know who you are?"

"Only if you read Perez Hilton. Instead you're reading... what? Elmo books? Or that series, the one with the parrot who protects the city from crime after school."

Surprise makes me laugh. "Sometimes. I'm surprised you even know about the parrot."

The taller one points to the older one. "He was on an off-Broadway production based on the children's book series. Chicago Tribune called it subversive and funny."

"Very far off Broadway," the older one says with a wink. "Oliver Morrison at your service. And this is my brother, Lucas. Nothing the blogs write about us is ever true. We've tried emailing them, but they insist on snapping unflattering photos of us at Walgreens."

"Our claim to fame is our parents, really." He

names a super popular actor and actress.

"Oh," I say. "I didn't even know they were married."

They exchange another look. "They weren't. Anyway, we don't want to talk about ourselves. We've done that lots of times already. We want to talk about you."

"I'm not interesting. No famous actors or actresses in my family line. No off-Broadway plays. No tabloids or blogs or Instagrams or anything really. I'm just a regular girl."

"A regular girl who Beau Rochester can't stop staring at."

I glance at him, and sure enough, he's staring right at me. Our eyes meet across the room. Zoey is practically in his lap, which I think can't be good for his leg, but I'm certainly not going to move her. There are invisible strings that pull me toward him, even as I'm standing still. I can feel the gravity from him, though whether he's the planet and I'm the star or the other way around, I don't know. In his dark eyes I see his frustration with the dinner party small talk, the lingering pain from his leg, his intense desire to get a whiskey neat.

The only person I actually recognize is a famous Latino actor, but I would never want to presume. What if I'm wrong? What if I think it's him just because he's ridiculously good looking? Everyone looks different in a Maine sitting room compared to a red-carpet photo.

Mrs. Fairfax appears in the doorway. "Dinner's served."

The group makes their way to the dining room. I gather Paige from the bar cart where someone's been mixing elaborate drinks. She's fascinated by the striations in color, one drink full of sunset oranges and yellows with a hint of purple, another with alternating blue and green layers. It's probably not the best part of her education that she learns about cocktail mixing, but at least she's not drinking them. She just wants to rest her chin on the cart and watch them the same way you'd do for a lava lamp.

"Come on," I tell her. "Time to eat dinner."

She makes a face, and I know she's thinking of the weird food. Now I'm a little nervous about it, too. Not because I don't think I'll like it, but I'm not sure what my reactions will be. These people have probably tried every food under the sun. This is the most exotic meal I've ever had, and it's surely mundane to them.

Zoey appears at my side. "You didn't drink your wine. You didn't like it?"

I glance at the large amount of red liquid left. "Oh… umm, not really. I'm sorry. I'm sure it's great wine. Maybe I'm not a wine person."

She beams a sympathetic smile. "It's not for everyone. We have an incredible vodka. It goes down so smooth you barely even know it's there."

"I'm not sure I'm a vodka person either."

"Don't worry. You'll love it. Come on, you can sit right next to me. I'll make sure you're well taken care of. I want you to have a good time now that you've crashed our little party."

CHAPTER TWENTY
Jane Mendoza

A LCOHOL HAS ALWAYS been associated with pain.

When my foster father would drink, he'd get violent. Noah drinks, too, but he just gets depressed when he has a few beers. There's nothing good that happens. And it tastes terrible. A little splash of coconut Bacardi in my Coke was the most I could handle at parties.

I would have preferred plain Coke, honestly. The rum made it taste weird.

That tastes nothing like the imported top-shelf vodka in lemon drops. I drink them down like it's rainwater and I've been dying of thirst. They're delicious. And I'm drunk.

Being drunk is amazing.

It's not about pain. Everything feels so good right now.

Paige went to sleep hours ago. I took her upstairs feeling woozy as we climbed the steps and

I helped her into bed. I could have stayed there. I would have stayed there, but Oliver and Lucas Morrison, or as I call them, the Hemsworth brothers, invaded my room with dry humor and coaxed me downstairs again.

Turns out the famous actor was actually Mateo Garza. *The* Mateo Garza. The one who was in all those superhero movies. I found that out when someone casually called him Mateo and asked about his filming schedule. I would be starstruck if I wasn't busy being tipsy.

I've had two lemon drops. Maybe three. Or four?

It doesn't matter. The important thing is that everyone should know how great this feels. I tell that to Lucas, who thinks that's hilarious. They're both pretty tipsy, too.

And possibly high. Most of the dinner party guests have taken turns in the bathroom. Doing snow, Oliver informs me under his breath. Only Mr. Rochester and Zoey haven't taken that trip. Oh, and me. I don't have any snow. That makes me laugh.

"What's so funny?" Oliver asks.

"I don't know." There are tears in my eyes. "I love you guys. You know that? You're my best friends."

That sets off another round of us laughing. At some point in the evening we moved back into the room with the fireplace. It's just so big and warm and fiery. I love this room.

"Jane." That's Lucas. His eyes are super blue. "I'm going to suggest something. I don't want to shock you, but I think you're really hot. We both do."

I giggle, though I don't know why it's funny. There doesn't need to be a reason. Everything's funny right now. "I think you're hot, too," I whisper.

Oliver puts his arm around my shoulders. "Invite us up to your room."

"You already saw my room," I say, drawing the word out. It sounds funny. Kind of like vroom. "Room. Room. It's not interesting."

"It's very interesting with you in it. There's a small bed, but I bet we could all fit."

"All three of us," I say, fascinated by the idea. The bed is way too small for all of us, but what if we shrunk? "We would be so tiny. Little elf people all lined up in that bed."

Lucas's shoulders are shaking with laughter. I can feel him moving the whole sofa. Oliver's not laughing, though. He takes my chin in his hand and turns me to face him. His lips press against mine. I suck in a breath of shock. He uses the opening to press his tongue inside my mouth. It pushes against my teeth, demanding entry. I make a small sound of distress.

"What are you doing?" I say, pulling back.

"Having a good time," he says with an easy grin, his lids low.

Lucas's hand rests on my thigh. His fingers are between my legs. Not touching all the way in a private part, but close. So close. "We both want to feel good, Jane. You can make us feel good. We'll make you feel good, too."

My throat feels thick and swollen. There's a strange taste in my mouth. The taste of Oliver. The imprint of him. It's not unpleasant, but it's not… Mr. Rochester. It's not Beau. "You're talking about sex."

"Sex with both of us," Oliver says, pulling me in for a hug. "We like to share."

Like a Tonka truck. That's the first thing I think of—two brothers sharing a Tonka truck. That makes me break into a fit of giggles, but the men don't take offense. They chuckle along with me. Then Oliver's hand moves down my arm. His fingertips graze the outside of my breast. Lucas pushes his hand closer to the top of my thighs. "Invite us upstairs, Jane."

No, I don't want them to come upstairs. It's cold up there. And the bed is way too small for us. Plus I don't want to have sex with them. They're not Beau.

"I don't know," I whisper, leaning my head on Oliver's shoulder. "You're so pretty."

He's pretty like one of those marble sculptures you see in textbooks from the ancient Greeks. You don't think about getting into bed with a marble sculpture.

It would not feel soft and cuddly.

Oliver pulls me in for another kiss; his palm covers my breast. I gasp in surprise, but then Lucas's hand delves deep between my legs, almost touching my sex. It's so much. It's so much, and it's not actually funny.

I'm not laughing anymore.

"Get the hell out of my house."

Everything stops.

Oliver pulls back, only slightly. He's still embracing me. "What the fuck?" he asks in this tone that manages to be both friendly and offended.

Mr. Rochester sits in the armchair, leaned back, casual as ever. The only sign that he's serious is the flashing in his dark eyes and the ferocity in his voice. "You heard me."

We all know that he has three broken bones in his body. That he underwent major surgery only a few nights ago, and yet there's a sense of lingering violence in the air.

A warning crackling like static before a storm.

"We were just having a little fun." Oliver.

"And now it's over. You have five minutes to vacate the premises."

It's only now, when everyone stands still that I realize how far things got in a room full of strangers. There are other people in close embraces. I don't think we were the only ones making out, but it's still crazy. And not funny. Like suddenly nothing is funny anymore. I'm so sad about it. It feels like nothing might ever be funny again.

Zoey stands up. "Beau. You don't mean this."

"You too," he says without glancing at her.

Her mouth opens. Her shock feels genuine. I feel bad for her, even though I think she got me really drunk on purpose. "Don't make her leave," I say. "It's raining outside."

"It's always raining outside," Mr. Rochester says.

"It was a kiss," Zoey says, her voice rising in pitch. "They kissed her. Are you that much of a caveman that you can't stand to see anyone kiss her?"

A sigh. "I don't expect you to understand, Zoey."

"What's that supposed to mean?"

"It means you never cared much about fidelity. Go back to LA. I don't want you here."

There's a terrible crack. It happens without anything changing in the physical scene. It's only a feeling—the knowledge that her confidence snaps in half. Her assurance that she's welcome, the beautiful facade she presents the world, gone.

"Let's get out of here," Mateo says. He speaks softly, but everyone seems to listen. Their shock evaporates and changes to a directed energy.

In the next moment Zoey lifts her chin. "Fine," she says, haughty as a queen. "Clearly Beau wants to fuck his pretty little nanny. We shouldn't interrupt time that he's already paid for."

Oliver mutters to his brother across me. "We can probably console her back at the inn."

A soft grunt of agreement. Lucas gives me a kiss on the cheek. "I'll think of you fondly, darling girl. And imagine that you're her until I black out."

It takes some rustling around, some searching for shoes and jackets, and then eventually they're gone. I lean back on the sofa and throw out my arms. The leather feels so blessedly good against my skin. "I think she was calling me a prostitute," I say to the empty room.

"Don't worry about her," the room says. No, it's not the room talking. It's Mr. Rochester.

I turn my head to look at him. "You were mean to her."

"I'm mean to everyone."

"Not Paige."

He raises one eyebrow. "Maybe not her."

"It's such a relief," I tell him soberly. "If you were mean to her, I don't know what I'd do. She's gone through enough losing her parents without some guy being cruel."

"Like your foster father was cruel?"

I bite my lip. "I don't like to talk about that."

"I made it so that they couldn't foster anymore. Maybe it was worse than I imagined. Should I turn the district attorney on him? Or maybe I should just fly down there and kick his ass."

"Don't be silly," I say, giving him a grin. "You couldn't kick anyone's ass. Your leg is broken."

He lifts a walking stick that he's been using to get around tonight. "That's what this is for."

"You know the doctor told you not to use

crutches. That's not even crutches. That's worse than crutches. You're going to open your wound back up and not heal properly. And then what am I going to do with you? Not bring you food, that's for sure. You can beg Zoey to come back."

His lips quirk. "You're bossy when you're drunk."

"I'm bossy all the time. I just can't tell you what I'm really thinking all the time."

"I want to hear what you're really thinking."

I roll my eyes. "You're just saying that now because you've had whiskey and everything seems funny. Once we're sober you're going to be a grumpy boss man again."

"A grumpy boss man?" He's clearly holding back laughter.

I stand up because he can't. Then I'm leaning on the arm of his chair, the same way Zoey did. The leather's still warm from her butt. Mr. Rochester has to look up at me this way.

We're so close. So close I can feel the heat coming from his body.

It's hotter than the fireplace.

I look him directly in the eyes. The dark gaze reflects the flames. "I'd say, shove it up your ass. And then you'd say, you're fired, Jane."

"You want to tell me to shove it up your ass?"

"Then again maybe we can just get drunk every day. Then you'd never be angry. And I'd never have to be sad again."

He tugs me onto his lap, and I squirm, trying to avoid hurting his leg with my weight. Only then do I feel something hard that's definitely not his leg. "You're always sad. And the worst part is, I want to make you happy. I promised myself I'd never go down this road again."

"Because of the woman you loved before."

"No," he murmurs against my neck, and I realize we're even closer than I thought. We're all wrapped up in each other. He's holding my waist and my leg. I've got my arms on his shoulders. "I didn't love her. I wanted her, and I almost broke myself trying to have her."

"You built a billion-dollar company trying to win her."

"And how do you think you build those? By becoming someone ambitious, someone cold and hard, someone unethical. I didn't even recognize myself by the end."

I pull back and push a lock of dark hair from his forehead. Part of me knows I would never do this if I weren't drunk. The other part of me doesn't care. It feels good. Maybe it would always have felt good, if I'd have had the courage to do it before. "The playboy Beau Rochester."

"Yes."

"The one who had sex with lots of supermodels."

His hand tightens in my hair. "Did you like when they touched you?"

I blink slowly. It takes me a second to realize what he means. "They made me laugh."

"But did you like it when they touched you?"

My forehead leans against his. "They weren't you."

"You break me apart."

I press my lips against his. The other times we were together, in his study and outside Paige's room, he initiated it. I enjoyed what he did, but I was passive. Obedient, even. Good little Jane Mendoza who does what she's told.

This is another side of me. The ocean during a storm.

I'm the one crossing boundaries tonight.

CHAPTER TWENTY-ONE
BEAU ROCHESTER

JANE SITS ON my lap. It shouldn't feel so good, not with my leg aching and my heart heavy. But of course my cock is hard as iron. It has no problem with the idea of fucking her even though I ignored her for the past few days.

She doesn't seem to have a problem with the idea either.

Her hands keep running through my hair, and it feels so good I close my eyes and turn my head toward her like some wild animal being tamed by a fairy. She's surrounding me—her touch, her scent. It's only because she's drunk. I shouldn't take advantage of her. I shouldn't, but I'm upside down in the dark water, unable to breathe.

I turned my back on her, and now I'm going to drown.

"You don't really want me," I tell her. She wants safety, and she thinks I can give that to her. But I can't. It's a mirage. I'm no more capable of being the man she needs than the cliff itself. We are both impenetrable, indestructible. Made that way through decades of erosion.

Because she's drunk, that makes her giggle. "You don't know what I want."

"Then tell me, sweet girl."

She puts her hands on my head on either side and looks me right in the eye. I don't know whether she's doing it to appear very serious or whether she just can't focus on me. I shouldn't have let Zoey serve her drinks. "I want the fourth thing. What's number four?"

I lost every principle I held dear building my shipping company, trying to win Emily Macom, trying to become more than the dirt-poor son of a lobsterman.

Who the hell am I now? That's what I asked myself.

I swore that I'd never need anything so badly again. Then this young woman sits on my lap and asks for number four. Number fucking four. As if there's a little kama sutra book sitting on her nightstand that she's working through, ever the diligent straight A student.

And I'm helpless against her wishes.

You're making a real sacrifice here, Rochester.

I drop my head back in the armchair. "You're

too drunk."

"And you're not the boss. You don't get to make the decision for me."

She's adorable. And technically incorrect. I am the boss. "We should wait."

"So you can come up with more excuses?"

A bark of laughter. "I don't need excuses not to touch you. God, look at you. In a T-shirt and jeans, looking more sexy and elegant than anyone else in the room."

"Oh yeah? Prove it."

She has a mouth on her, that's for sure. I do enjoy her submission, but if she were only ever meek, it would not be enough. I like when she challenges me.

I take her small, delicate hand and put it on my throbbing cock. There are layers of cloth between her skin and mine, but pleasure still pulses through me. "This proof enough?"

She starts to slide off my lap, but I stop her. "Nope."

An adorable pout. "I thought you liked it."

"No, sweetheart. I fucking loved it, but we're not doing that tonight."

She bites her lip and strokes her hand along my cock. It may have been her first blowjob, but she learned fast. "I liked what we did before."

"That was number three. We're moving on to number four tonight."

Her dark eyes hold the depth of the ocean. "What's number four?"

"Get over there to the couch."

She picks herself up off me and walks to the couch.

Then she sits there looking prim and a little nervous. This is what she would have looked like if she were local to me and had come over for an interview. This is how she looked in the video interview from the agency. I would like to say I didn't imagine her sucking my dick while watching her talk about getting straight As, but that would be a lie.

I didn't think it would actually happen, though.

"Take off your shirt."

She pulls it over her head. None of the hesitation from last time. Maybe she's getting comfortable with me. Or maybe she's just drunk. I should put her to bed without touching her, but instead I'm going to make her feel good.

"Now your jeans."

They fall to the floor. She stands there in her bra and panties, firelight licking at her bronze skin. I want to worship her. I want to ride her.

She wakes every instinct in my body.

"Do you want this, Jane?"

A guileless gaze. "When I'm with you, I forget everything else."

I laugh a little at myself, only internally. For wanting a different answer. For wanting something with me, Beau Rochester, son of a lobsterman, entrepreneur, playboy, and now uncle. Instead she wants release, and doesn't she fucking deserve it? "Sit down and spread your legs."

She does. It's a little awkward, but that makes it sweeter.

I stand up. My leg puts up a strong protest. Agony streaks through me—not only the actual wound but through my entire body. I lean on the walking stick and make my way over to her. It's inelegant in the extreme, the way I manage to kneel without blacking out from the pain.

None of that matters when I'm looking at her pussy.

It's covered with her white underwear, which has gone damp.

"I think it did make you hot," I tell her. "Oliver and Lucas touching you."

"Maybe." It's a whispered confession.

"It's okay. You have nothing to be ashamed

about." I'm the one who's ashamed. For letting Zoey into this house, into my bedroom. For doing it to make Jane jealous. I didn't fuck Zoey, but I let Jane think I did, and that's the worst part. "They would have made you feel good. They'd have taken you back to their room and fucked you. They like it in both your pussy and your ass. Would you have given them that?"

She shifts on the leather, half uncomfortable, half turned on. "I don't know."

"You'd feel good in the moment. They'd make sure of that. Only after you'd be sore." I tap on the placket of her panties. "You can, you know? You could have gone with them for the night. I don't own this pussy. I don't own your body."

"It feels like you do."

My cock flexes against my boxer briefs. It likes that idea. A lot. Tonight isn't about my cock. "Yeah. You like being owned? Possessed? You like being told what to do?"

"Yes." The word is almost a moan.

"You liked it when you had to rub your pussy on my shoe, didn't you?"

"It was so wrong. So humiliating."

"And it made you hotter than ever. Your mouth full of my cock. Your pussy juice covering my shoes. You were desperate to come, weren't you? My good little nanny."

I tug her panties down her legs and then push them apart. She's so pink. So swollen. Fuck, she'd feel amazing around my cock. No. No, this is for her.

When I'm with you, I forget everything else. That's what this is about.

Her bra covers her breasts. They're not particularly large. Not particularly small. This middle size. This in-between that should be unremarkable. And yet, they're perfect. A goddamn revelation. I push the fabric aside, so her breasts jut out. The bunched-up bra cups push her up, cup her the way my hands want to. I tweak her nipple, making her moan.

I press my face against the inside of her thigh. She jumps, still nervous about this.

"No one ever tasted you, did they?"

She already said she hadn't given a blowjob, but it doesn't mean for sure that no one did this. Her dark gaze holds mine while she shakes her head.

I'm the first. The only, some primal part of my brain demands. I spread her with my fingers, watching her open for me, petal by petal. She would have let me lick her pussy regardless of the alcohol. But she might not have done it in a room lit by lamps and fire. For that I have to thank, ironically, Zoey. I only let her plan this fucking dinner party because I was curious. Curious to see what Jane would make of my old friends. Curious to see what they'd make of her.

Turns out they want to fuck her. Funny, that it should bother me so much.

I give one long lick from base to top. It's the warmup, but it's so intimate, so delicious, that I groan. How am I going to last through this? My comfort doesn't matter. My aching leg. My throbbing cock. None of it has anything to do with my tongue against her clit.

She sucks in a breath, her body rocking gently with desire.

I pull her hips to the edge of the couch so that I can lick her deep. I slide my tongue into her pussy and bite down gently on her outer flesh. She lets out a small keening sound. Then I push a finger inside—God, she's tight. So swollen with arousal. I have to force my way in. I lick my way to her clit and then flutter my tongue over the sensitive bud.

It makes her ass come off the couch. She rocks against my face in urgent abandon. "Please, please, please."

The way she begs makes me want to give her everything. I hold back. I could suck her clit and reach her G-spot and make her come right away. That would shortchange her. It wouldn't make her forget everything, so instead I continue a soft flutter. I spell out words with my tongue. Beautiful, I tell her. Perfect. Mine. I write across her clit with soft swipes that make her thighs quiver. Her hands come to my hair, and she yanks. She yanks hard enough that it distracts me from my leg, and I grunt in satisfaction.

My arms wrap underneath her thighs, holding her in place so I can fuck her with my mouth. I give her long licks again, letting her cool down for a minute, letting the urgency drop for just a second so I can build her back up. She cries in protest. "Beau."

"Now I'm Beau again, huh?"

"Yes." She hisses the word while pumping her hips toward me.

I'm messy with her. My lips are wet from her lust. I lick them and then go back for more. Her breathing fills the room, a counterpoint to the crackle and pop of the fire.

"Let me come. Please."

"Not yet."

"Oh God, it hurts. It hurts not to come."

Maybe I'm drawing it out to punish her. Or

maybe I just need her to feel as good as she'd have felt with Lucas and Oliver. Better than that. She could have gone with them and had a night to remember. They are famous in LA—and Prague, and Tokyo, and London—for their exploits. They could have taught her things, but I want her here—quivering under my lips.

That's the kind of experience she can have later. The kind she will have later, when she leaves me. Because inevitably she'll leave. I'll be here, covered in sea spray, drenched in rain, freezing to death on the cliffs of Maine. Later, later. Right now she's here. With me. I show my gratitude by pushing two fingers inside this time. I reach deep, finding the spot that makes her jolt. And then I rub it again. And again. She's moaning now, seconds from coming. It's getting harder to stop her. Harder to draw this out.

She's on a razor's edge, vibrating with how close she is. God, she's magnificent. Her breasts shake. Her thighs tense. Her hand fists in my hair, demanding that I worship her.

I press the flat of my tongue against her clit at the same time as I twist my fingers inside her. She comes with a sharp cry, her whole body writhing. Darkness and chaos. Water in my lungs. I breathe the salt and musk of her deep, wanting to remember this for a cold future night.

CHAPTER TWENTY-TWO

JANE MENDOZA

THE DOORBELL RINGS at noon.

I open it without checking the peephole. I'm hoping it's the event company come to pick up their china and silverware and sashes. Zoey is the one who made the order, and without information from her, I have no idea how to return them.

"Holy shit. You're Mateo Garza."

A casual smirk that probably earns him a zillion dollars per second on film. He's wearing a plain blue T-shirt and jeans, but he might as well have just stepped off some fancy men's magazine cover. "We met yesterday. You're Jane, right? The nanny."

"Yeah, but I thought I might have imagined it. I got a little tipsy."

"Top-shelf vodka will do that."

"Good thing I can't afford it, then. Because my head hurts this morning."

A small, sympathetic laugh. "I think we're all feeling the hangover this morning."

I open the door wider. "You're here to see Mr. Rochester?"

"Yeah. Though I wanted to check on you, too."

I glance behind me, just in case. Empty foyer. "Me?"

"Can we chat for a minute?"

"You want to talk to me? The nanny? Do you need tips on diaper changing, because I have to warn you right now, I don't actually do that."

He gives a genuine laugh then. "Come take a walk with me."

After a beat of disbelief, I shake my head. Then I peek into the kitchen, where Paige is diligently sweeping her paintbrush across the printed worksheets. This is the next stage of virtual learning for her. We've moved on from rocks and tree stumps, but we still use paint. "I'm going to step outside, honey. Be back in ten minutes, okay? Try to finish the math worksheet by then, because then we have a bumblebee to color."

Beau was really not kidding about their garden obsession.

I follow him outside, along the rocky trail that

leads along the cliff. We look at the ocean. It's a tame day. No rain. No thunder. Just the normal wild action of the waves. "Pretty," he says.

My hands go to my pockets. It's a little chilly, but I didn't bother to put on a jacket. I didn't think we'd be talking for that long. "Honestly, why am I here?"

"I've known Beau a long time."

"Oh." That's interesting, since I've developed a major crush on my boss. Though I'm not sure how I can ever speak to him again after last night. It still doesn't answer why Mateo Garza wants to talk to me alone. I glance up at his study. There's no shadow. As far as I can see, he isn't watching us walk. Which is good. Hopefully he's in bed, letting his leg heal.

He continues walking, and I follow along. "I knew him back when he was starting his company. I was still doing open-call auditions back then. We were broke, basically."

"No top-shelf vodka?"

"No top-shelf vodka. That came later, for both of us. The truth is I hold myself responsible for getting him into the party scene. Those are my people."

Part of me wants to defend Mr. Rochester. Beau. He can choose his own friends. The other part of me acknowledges that he was an outsider last night. Even though he fit in—he had the money, the connections, everything they wanted from him. He didn't enjoy himself there. "Why are you telling me this?"

"Because he partied pretty hard after he sold his company. I'm not sure he ever really recovered. Then he got the call about Paige. Now you're here."

"I'm the nanny. That's all."

He gives me a *get real* look.

"Listen," I say, stopping to turn and face him. "I'm sure you're a very nice person. And it seems like you actually care about Mr. Rochester. And you're this massive heartthrob guy that most girls would kill to meet. But he doesn't need you to protect him from me."

"Is that what you think I'm doing?"

"I get that I'm a broke nobody, so you think I'm after him for his money."

"It would be one way to earn a living."

"Or maybe you think I want to get some story that I can sell to the tabloids. Which is crazy. I mean for one thing, I've signed a nondisclosure agreement. For another thing, that's just mean."

"It's mean," he says, repeating me.

"I wouldn't do that even if I hadn't signed an

agreement."

"Maybe I am a little jaded. It's been a while since I heard someone who wouldn't do something for money or advancement because it was mean."

"Both you and Mr. Rochester are jaded," I tell him, crossing my arms.

"It's possible I feel guilty about some of the hard partying he did. I hooked him up with that scene. I'm from here." He nods across the water. "We moved to California together. He lived in San Francisco and I lived in LA, but we'd hang out together most weekends. He worked eighty-hour weeks Monday through Friday and he needed some connection to Maine."

I'm quiet, hoping he'll continue. It's a surprise to me that he knew Beau before he got rich and famous. I suppose that means he knew Beau's brother, too.

He looks up at the sky. "Then Emily married Rhys. It changed Beau. Hardened him. He got into the party scene. Sex. Drugs. The whole thing."

"Until Paige. He doesn't do that now." I suppose he still has sex, if you count what we did in his study. Which Mateo probably does. I'm not going to mention that part, though.

"I wasn't trying to protect him from you," Mateo says, sounding grim. "I was trying to protect you from him. You seem nice. And innocent. You don't know what kind of man he is, what kinds of secrets he has. You should walk away."

Part of me wants to ask about the secrets.

That would prove his point, though.

"I hope I'm nice, but I'm not as innocent as you think. I've seen bad things in the world."

Bad things happened when my mother died of an overdose when I was five. I found her on the floor in the kitchen and waited for hours for my dad to come home.

My dad had his heart attack at work.

He kissed me on the forehead one day before school and never came back.

Bad things happened in foster homes for years.

Some I got pulled out of. Some I didn't.

Mateo studies me. He has these eyes that are light brown, almost as if I can see deep inside his soul. I don't know whether it's part of his beauty or whether he really carries some old wisdom. Either way it feels like he understands what I'm saying. And what I'm *not* saying.

"I believe you," he says, his voice gentle. I can

imagine him just like this on a cliff somewhere with a green screen behind him instead of a gorgeous hazy day. He would be playing the part of a concerned friend. Except this is real. Or is it? "He's not the obvious kind of bad. He's the kind that sneaks up on you. The kind you don't see in the fog until it's too late."

"Is that right?" comes Mr. Rochester's voice. It carries across the wind. I jump and turn. He's standing a few yards back, leaning heavily on his walking stick. "I was wondering what Mateo Garza and Jane Mendoza would have to chat about out here. Now I know."

Mateo steps in front of me, as if protecting me from his anger. "Don't blame her."

"I don't," Mr. Rochester says, biting off the words. "It's crystal clear what's happening here. I turn my back for one second, and now you're trying to get into her pants."

"That's not what happened," I say, my voice soothing, unable to keep silent.

Dark eyes flash at me. "Now you're on his side?"

"I'm not on anyone's side! I just don't want you walking around. Is that honestly too much to ask? Can you follow the doctor's orders for like a full twenty-four hours?"

"You are fooling yourself if you think he doesn't want a night with you."

I gesture broadly. "This is Mateo Garza. Maybe you've been friends with him forever, so you missed the memo where he can have anyone. Why would he want me?"

"Don't undersell yourself," Mr. Rochester says, but it doesn't sound flattering. "He's had his fill of actresses and models. Now he wants the real deal."

"I think it's the pain meds," I mutter to Mateo. "He refuses to take them."

"He's not entirely wrong." Mateo has this perfect expression of handsome sheepishness. Did he perfect the look in order to get parts? Or did he get parts because he was born with that look? "I did think about asking you for coffee, but that doesn't mean what I'm saying isn't true."

I rub both hands over my face. The chill is getting to me. "You," I tell Mr. Rochester. "Should be inside, with your leg up, taking pain medicine. And you," I tell Mateo. "Thank you for the visit, but honestly, I'm fine. You're *more* than fine, but I would have to pass on coffee."

Grass crunches under my feet as I stalk away. Am I crazy for just turning down a potential coffee date with Mateo Garza? I still can't quite believe he was interested in me. No, it seemed like they had some kind of testosterone war going on.

Mr. Rochester got jealous about Oliver and Lucas, too. It's kind of a thing with him. It makes me wonder if he got cheated on at some point.

Still fuming, and confused, I bang open the front door and take off my boots. I bypass the kitchen and head into one of the sitting rooms. The one where Mr. Rochester and I spent an evening together. Where I spread my legs and he licked me until I came.

I avoid the sofa but instead sit on the large armchair.

After a minute small feet pad behind me.

A mop of dirty blonde hair appears by my side. Along with an impish grin. She doesn't say anything as she climbs onto the chair with me, using my arm, my shoulder, my legs, as her personal jungle gym. Some of my frustration fades. Children have that magic.

"What's wrong?" she asks.

"Nothing." I make a funny face to distract her. "I just have a lot on my mind."

"What did that man want from you?" The distraction failed.

"Oh, he came to the dinner party last night. Do you remember him? He just wanted to talk to me about something real quick. Grown-up things."

That earns me a massive eye roll. Honestly, the attitude on this six-year-old. I don't even know what's going to happen when she becomes a teenager. Will she create more attitude? Or is that impossible? I shouldn't find it so endearing. My heart sinks. I won't know her then. "Grown-up things. Mommy was always talking about grown-up things. I couldn't be in the room."

Caution invades me, but I focus on looking casual. She doesn't bring up her mother very often. And she brings up her father even less. I have to tread carefully. I googled some articles on how to deal with children with grief. It said to let them open up when they were ready. Don't push but don't shut down the conversation if they want to talk, either.

"What is so interesting about grown-up stuff?" she asks. "I saw Mommy's diary one time and it was all about B says this and R says that. So much talking."

I'm torn by emotion—amusement that she found her mother's diary so boring, grief that she'll never get to see her mother again. I wonder if I'm supposed to chastise her for reading something she clearly shouldn't. "Maybe that's what makes it grown-up stuff," I say lightly. "Only grown-ups like it. And only kids like kid stuff."

She considers this. "But you're a grown-up, and you like my stuff. Don't you?"

I didn't like it when Beau Rochester called me young and naive. I didn't particularly like it when Mateo Garza called me innocent, either. Maybe every nineteen-year-old woman wants to seem older. We can vote and have sex. We can enlist in the military. In so many ways we are grown, but in other ways we aren't. "Maybe I'm in between," I say, which is a big concession. I have all the responsibilities of being a grown-up, but I have the desire to play. "And I do love our games. Painting and taking walks in the woods. I think I'm even getting better at Monopoly."

She giggles. "I can still beat you though."

"That's probably true," I concede. "What should we do for the rest of the day?"

It's Saturday, so we don't have to do more schoolwork. Even though there's still a backlog of worksheets from before I came here, I like to give her time off to rest and recharge.

Her head leans back on my forearm. I'm touched by the gentle trust she shows in me.

"I dunno. Maybe we could write in our diaries. Do you have one?"

"No," I say, drawing the word out. "But if I had one, you definitely couldn't read it."

She sticks her tongue out. Then she gets serious. "I don't know. Maybe Mommy did think someone would read her diary. She said that she thought someone would hurt her."

Goose bumps run over my skin. I have to work hard to keep my expression neutral. I've seen too much domestic violence in my life to pretend like this is nothing. "Did someone hurt you?"

Her gray eyes are solemn. She shakes her head without breaking our gaze. "But I wasn't with her when she died. What if someone did hurt her?"

My breath catches. All I know about her parents' deaths is the one article. A boating accident, it said. Could a boating accident have happened on purpose? Then why would they both have died? "I don't know. We could ask Uncle Beau about it. I'm sure he knows what happened."

"No way," she says. "I tried talking to him, and he told me I was wrong."

I suck in a breath. Mr. Rochester does have a rather abrupt way of handling things, especially messy, emotional things. "Maybe he felt too sad to talk about it then. We could try again. This is important. If you feel afraid, then we have to talk about it."

She tucks her head in my shoulder. Her dirty blonde hair covers her face. "You're the only person who talks to me anyway."

I plant a kiss on top of her head. "I know. It's hard for Uncle Beau to open up. He's not naturally very chatty, but I'm sure he'll learn."

"I don't just mean now. Before, too. Daddy was always working. And Mommy would leave for her trips. They never had time for me."

A wrench in my heart. I suppose it always feels like you'll have more time. Maybe they were terrible parents. Or maybe they were good parents who were just too wrapped up in their lives to see the moments running through their hands like sand. "Who would stay with you?"

"Mrs. Fairfax."

Oh. "I didn't realize she was your nanny before me."

A scrunched nose. "She didn't play with me or anything, but she made sure there was food."

I hide my cringe. That sounds like a bad situation for a child not yet six years old, to be alone in this house without a real caregiver. I wonder if Beau Rochester knew about what was happening with his niece while he was busy being a playboy.

For that matter I wonder where he even was after he stepped out of the limelight. "I appreciate you telling me this," I say to Paige. "You can always talk to me. I will never get mad at you for your feelings or for being honest, okay?"

She wriggles on my lap, and I wonder if we've lost the seriousness of the moment.

Then she leans close, her small arms wrapping around my neck in a hug. I squeeze her back and close my eyes, breathing her sweet child-scent in deep.

"I'm afraid," she whispers against my throat, and I tense. "Whoever hurt her might come to the cliff. They might come for me next." Before I can think of a reply, she jumps down off my lap and runs upstairs. When I follow her, she already has the Monopoly game out. She deals out the money and we play, pretending she didn't say what she said, my mind reeling.

She definitely can still beat me.

CHAPTER TWENTY-THREE
JANE MENDOZA

MY CONTRACT WITH the Bassett Agency technically gives me Sundays off, although there is a clause for the family to ask for more work if needed or to change the day. For the most part I've spent Sundays with Paige. I don't know anyone in Maine anyway, and I enjoy spending time with her. But this Sunday, I step into Beau's office.

"I'm going up to Portsmouth," I tell him, hoping my voice is casual. I'm already dressed for the excursion, in long sleeves, a puffy jacket vest, and a scarf. My boots are downstairs, and an Uber has been ordered. "For my day off."

He sits behind his desk and raises his brows. "You get days off?"

"Ha. You know I do."

"Fine. It's probably a good idea for me to spend time with the brat."

I hesitate, wondering how much I should tell

him about Paige. Or if I should tell him anything. "Has she ever spoken to a professional? Like a therapist, about her parents?"

His expression turns hard. "Why?"

"It might be a good idea. A lot of kids need help coping with grief."

"I thought you had her talking to that school person."

"That's been helping, but I mean something more specific to her parents. Her loss." I blow out a breath. "She told me yesterday that she was afraid."

It drops about five degrees in the room. "Afraid?" He looks both incredulous and slightly wounded, as if I've managed to shoot a bear. "Of me?"

"No," I assure him. At least I don't think so. "I guess she has the idea that someone hurt her mom? And her dad? I didn't know what happened enough to say anything."

He stands abruptly and looks out the window. There's only gray. Gray like Paige's eyes. Not like Beau's though. His are dark brown. She must get hers from her mother's side. "Find someone," he says, his voice clipped. "No, find the best. Whoever deals with children and grief. Make an appointment and get her in to see them. If you hit any walls, let me know."

Because he'd pull strings. Those famous-people, rich-people, privileged-people strings. I don't resent them now, though. I understand them. You do anything for the people you love. And in my small way, I love Paige. "I'll start looking for someone this afternoon when I'm back."

He glances at me. "So where are you going? A coffee date?"

The words are thrown out casually, but I know they're not casual at all. "No."

"Lunch?"

I glare at him. "Not that it's any of your business, but no. I'm not ever going to see Mateo Carter again unless he's on the big screen. Happy now?"

"Far from it."

"You have no right to be jealous, not when you're the one who invited those men over. And especially not when you won't say anything to me that's kind unless we're having sex."

"To be honest I didn't think I was kind while we were having sex, either."

I give an exasperated laugh. "Have a nice morning with Paige. You should play Monopoly with her. That should last a few hours at least."

"That little loan shark? She's terrifying."

I stick out my tongue. "And you're the guy who built a billion-dollar business before he turned thirty. Surely you can stop her from getting a monopoly across an entire side."

He looks unmoved. And contemplative. "My brother and me, we were always competitive. Really competitive. That Monopoly board Paige loves? That was ours from years ago. Half the games ended in physical violence."

"I feel like that's normal for Monopoly. It's not a nice game."

"It wasn't only that. If we raced, we would trip each other. If we were jumping off cliffs, we'd break an arm just to beat the other person. Everything was a competition."

"But you still loved each other."

"Did we?" He seems surprised by the idea. "We weren't a particularly loving family. Dad would shout at us. Mom would yell at us. Rhys and I would get into a fistfight before dinner. The irony is that he was better than me. Objectively. At everything. He was older, taller, stronger, smarter."

"I don't know. You're pretty smart."

He gives a huff of laughter. "I'm something. I don't know when to quit. That's what I bring to the table. And with Rhys. Even though he was bigger and stronger than me, if I just kept fighting, if I never quit, then sometimes I'd win."

"It probably helped you build that shipping business."

"Yeah. Probably."

"I'm also leaving her paint set by the door. Her brushes are clean."

"What would we do without you?" he asks, his tone serious.

A bright smile is my only defense. "I'm sure you'd get along fine."

I head downstairs to hide the ache in my chest. The truth is they would get along fine. Eventually. Not right away, but eventually they would stop arguing over Pop-Tarts and jackets.

They are family. I'm the hired help.

I can't get these things confused, even if my heart wants something else. That would be what Mateo warned me about. Beau Rochester would not set out to hurt me, but he could shatter me into pieces so easily. If I let myself get my hopes up, if I read more into his desire than is really there, I would fall for him. Eventually, I would fall apart.

When the Uber pulls up, I wave to Paige.

Mr. Rochester is a shadow behind her in the

window. It's the same Toyota Prius as before. The same driver. I wonder if he's the only one willing to drive up this crazy mountain.

"Do you come this way often?" I ask, mostly to see if he'll remember me.

"Nope."

Apparently not. We spend the drive in silence. I text a few people back home, including Noah. He sent me a meme of a lion who steals a wilderness photographer's camera. It's a joke. A reminder of one time when I took his hoodie from the laundry by mistake and then refused to give it back because it was so much warmer than mine. *One time*, I text back.

I don't have a specific plan for my day off. The agency deposited some money. Most of it gets held back. We're still a few months away from that payment, but there've been regular deposits every week that I haven't been spending. I haven't needed it for rent or food.

The Uber lets me out in front of shops. It's a strange feeling to know I could walk inside and buy something for myself, something fun and unnecessary, and still have enough to eat. Still have a roof over my head. Of course I really need to save it for when I start college.

One in five kids who age out of foster care

end up homeless. That could be me. That could be Noah or any of the other kids I grew up with. It will be one of them, which is why it's so important I go to college. Not only because I'll be able to help other kids in the system, but so that I can have security in my life. Safety. This is what survival looks like.

My phone rings, and I glance at the screen. Noah's grinning face looks up at me. My stomach does a little twist. I care about him like a brother. It hurts that we have this rift, but I don't know how to fix it beyond memes and one-line texts.

"Hey," I say, strolling down the sidewalk. There's an antique shop with these ceramic lions that look Chinese and a heavy screen that has Egyptian stuff drawn on it. I wonder how old something has to be before it's called antique.

"I've missed you," he says.

My heart squeezes. I pull back to check the time. "Aren't you at work?"

"I'm on break."

That means he's got fifteen minutes. Maybe less depending on if he needs a drink of water or to use the bathroom. The grocery store manager is strict about that. "I've missed you, too."

There's a whisper of air over the phone.

My eyes narrow. "Are you smoking?"

A short puff of laughter. "Jane."

"I thought we agreed no more smoking."

"That was before you moved to another state."

"I didn't move here. It's a temporary thing. You know that. I'm coming back to Houston." I only hope that we can resume our friendship when I do come back. It will hurt never to see Paige again. It will hurt never to see Beau Rochester again. "That's where I'm going to college."

There's another pause, and I know he's taking a drag of his cigarette. I hate that he feels like he needs them. They'll only make him sick, but I manage not to say that. "Sometimes I think it's better if you don't come back."

I stop walking. Only dimly I register that I'm stopped in front of a chowder restaurant with a giant clam on its hanging sign. "You don't mean that."

"You never fit in with us anyway."

I blink hard to fight the tears. "Stop it."

"It's true. We're all going to be on drugs or dead in fifteen years. Not you. You've got your eyes on something bigger. I want that for you."

I don't honestly know whether he's saying something he thinks will help me. Or if he's trying to hurt me. It wouldn't feel good to have your friend tell you you don't fit in, but as an orphan, as someone who's struggled with the concept of home for years, it's hell.

"I'm coming home to Houston," I tell him. "In six months. I hope we can still be friends then, but you need to stop acting like this. I don't miss this. I miss my old friend. I miss my brother. The one I could talk to about anything."

There's quiet. "What do you need to talk to him about?"

About Mr. Rochester. About Paige. "What do you think it means if a little girl is scared about the way her parents died? If she's worried they'll come back for her?"

"Sadness sometimes comes out as fear. Or anger. Remember that kid who thought his parents were astronauts who died in a secret mission to Mars?"

"But I just kept thinking, what if he was right? And no one believed him?"

A soft laugh. "Only you would possibly think that."

"This family has so many secrets, Noah."

"All families have secrets."

At the end of the street there's something large and gray bulging out from the grassy hill. A submarine, I realize as I get closer. Someone put a giant submarine in the middle of a park. USS Albacore, says a placard. I take a seat on a picnic bench nearby. "I don't know what to think. What to believe. I just need someone I can trust. I need you."

"You have me, Jane. I was talking shit because I was jealous."

"There seems to be a lot of that going around," I mutter.

"What?"

"You need to go, probably. Don't give Miller any excuses to dock your pay. And stop smoking."

"What would I do without you, Jane?"

I hang up, my heart still beating fast from the echo. What would he do without me? He'd get along fine if I never came back. Or maybe he'd be better off.

Sometimes I think it's better if you don't come back.

Mr. Rochester and Paige would be fine without me, too.

Which leaves me to wonder where I really belong.

My chest squeezes.

It's only here, with the breeze floating through my hair, a submarine rising at my back, that I realize why I actually took this day off.

Not because I wanted to get away from Mr. Rochester or Paige. Because I wanted to know who I was without them. As I sit here alone and slightly afraid, I know the answer.

I belong nowhere.

CHAPTER TWENTY-FOUR
JANE MENDOZA

W HEN I GET back to the house, it's past
dinner time. From the foyer I can hear the
strains of the sea shanty. Instead of the haunting
lullaby, it's coming out bright and sunny from a
six-year-old's mouth. "There was a light far away,"
she sings off key, "I followed the water's gift. But
when the night turned to day, I ended up adrift."

I find them in the kitchen, dancing around
the table. Paige waves a dish towel like a flag while
Beau makes grave ballroom steps around the
kitchen. They stop when they see me.

Paige grins. "You missed spaghetti."

"Oh no," I say lightly, ignoring the squeeze in
my heart. Imagine coming to this every night.
Imagine belonging in this scene. I don't, I don't.
"And I'm so hungry."

"There's leftovers in the fridge." Beau sounds
sardonic. "Compliments of the chef."

I glance at the clock on the oven. "It's time for

bedtime."

"Ah ah," he says. "Not on your day off."

"We have plans," Paige says, very serious. "Bedtime stories."

Another compression in the vicinity of my chest. It's a good thing they're spending time together. A good thing they're getting along. They may not need me, after all. "Okay."

Paige prances out of the room, waving her dish towel in precise movements only she understands. That leaves me alone with Beau. The day yawns between us, only a few hours apart. They felt like days. Weeks. Months. I'm getting too attached to him.

It makes me want to back away. For my own safety. My own protection.

Too late. I'm already in too deep.

"What's wrong?" he murmurs.

This family has so many secrets, Noah. "Nothing."

He shakes his head, a ghost of a smile still on his lips. "You make me insane, you know that? You make me want impossible things."

"Like what?" I'm already breathless. It's too tempting. He's too tempting.

"I want you, Jane."

Noah's words echo in my head. "You have

me."

It's true. Doesn't matter whether I want to belong to Beau Rochester. My heart made the decision a long time ago. My body, too. I wasn't consulted about the matter.

He frowns. "Then why do you look like someone died?"

"Will you come to me?"

His nostrils flare. "For what?" he asks, his voice low and gravelly. He knows exactly what I'm asking for, but he wants to make me say it. He'll probably make me beg before this is over. He'll have me on my knees, and worst of all, I'll want more.

My gaze meets his. "For number five."

His eyes darken. "Tonight?"

"Tonight." I want this to happen because I'm asking for it. I want this to happen in my own room. He already controls too much in our relationship.

"After I put Paige down for bed."

I leave the room, very aware that he's watching me go. Part of me wishes I'd worn something nicer than this pair of jeans and slouchy sweater, but the heat emanating from him leaves no question as to his thoughts.

Paige needs a bath. And a glass of water.

And bedtime stories.

I have a few hours to wait. I spend them taking a long shower. Shave. Moisturize. Everything more meaningful than anytime I've done it before, because Beau will see me like this. He'll touch me like this. The other times we've touched have been unplanned. This is different. This is my decision, start to finish. It's at once empowering and terrifying.

I stand near the bed, feeling nervous as hell.

Why did I make that offer? It's true that I want to sleep with him.

But I'm afraid. Afraid of what he'll think of me after. Afraid of what I'll think of myself. Afraid of the phantom memories who haunt this house. I'm so tired of being afraid.

"Jane."

I whirl and face him. He's standing in the doorframe, holding on to the top. It pulls his sweater up, revealing a small stretch of taut abs. My gaze soaks it in. I want him.

And it feels good, this wanting.

When I meet his eyes again, he has a knowing look. This is a man who knows his value. Who knows his worth. Who knows how to please a woman.

"I'm glad you're my first," I say impulsively,

and he freezes.

"Excuse me?"

"I thought—" I stammer. "I thought you knew I was a virgin."

He takes his time walking into the room, closing the door, and locking it. That seems promising, at least. He hasn't left. "I wondered, though I couldn't be sure. Some girls have sex but they don't give a blowjob."

"Oh no, I meant I hadn't done either of them before."

He drags me against his body. "You're shaking."

I let out an uneven breath. "I'm nervous."

"Do you think I'm going to hurt you?"

"No." Not the way he means. Not with his body. He has a massive amount of strength in those arms and abs and legs, but he would never use them against me. I trust him that much, but I know better than to trust him with my heart. Or do I?

He leans down to press a kiss to my forehead. "Then what?"

I'm nervous for a thousand reasons. It's hard to distill it into words. "That I won't be enough for you. You've been with models and actresses and—"

"God, Jane. Feel how much I want you." Both of his hands grasp my ass. He pulls me hard against him, our bodies flush, his erection painfully thick.

The shock of it, the intimacy of it, makes me gasp. "Not Zoey?"

A rueful laugh. "I deserve that. Not Zoey."

Not Emily? I don't have the courage to ask that question.

He captures my mouth, one hand holding my jaw, the other still holding my ass. His lips are warm and soft and probing. It's a question, this kiss. He's asking whether I really want this. Whether I'm sure. And I love that he's taking time to find out.

I answer with my own version of a kiss—mine demanding and certain.

He grunts in response.

The masculine sound of pleasure makes my thighs clench together.

"Do you have a condom?" Seven out of ten girls who age out of the foster care system will become pregnant before the age of twenty-one. I'm not going to let that happen, no matter how lost in him I get.

"Of course," he says, walking me back toward the bed. His hands explore me beneath my sweater, and my nipples become hard. He tugs the thick fabric off me, and cool air breathes across my skin. I suck in a breath, nervous now that he's seeing me fully naked.

His lids drop low. He looks at me with something like awe. He touches my breasts with reverence. There's worship in every breath he takes.

He takes off my jeans next, pushing down my panties along with them. I'm naked when I step out of the bunched fabric. Naked, and he's fully dressed. He drops his head and places kisses across my shoulder. His hand goes behind my back, lifting me up so he can suck my nipple. The warmth of his mouth makes me groan and buck my hips. It's an invitation. He slides his hand down to my pussy. Two fingers make their way inside me.

"Oh God," I whisper, tugging at his dark hair.

"I want you to come," he murmurs against my breast. "I want to feel you wet and clenching around my fingers. That way I'll know you're ready for me."

"I don't know if I can—"

A low rumble of a laugh. His fingers press deeper inside me. His thumb finds my clit. He rubs circles that make me stand on my tiptoes.

"You can."

The pleasure washes over me in waves. My legs can't support myself anymore, and he eases me down onto the bed. The same plain bedspread I saw when I walked into the room for the first time. How could I have imagined it would lead to this? I feel the stitching against my back. I'm hypersensitive. I can trace the veins of the bed against my back.

He follows me down, supporting himself on his elbow, his other hand still working between my legs. I squeeze my thighs together. "It's too much."

He shakes his head, inexorable. It's like arguing with a mountain. "You're still too tight. You need to come again. Let me make you feel good."

The words unlock something in me, and I sigh a relief built up over years. My head falls back over his arm, exposing my neck. He licks me there. Bites me there. Then his mouth closes over my other nipple. He sucks gently while his hand brings me closer and closer to orgasm. It's like my body is fighting it, fighting against a tidal wave, destined to lose.

He's making words with his tongue, writing across my breasts, embossing something into my skin. Mine, he writes. Then he bites down on the side of my breast, the flesh there soft and sensitive. I buck against his hand, and then I come in a hard gush, the climax wrapped around me like barbed wire, squeezing, hurting, drawing blood in certain places.

He's still stroking me gently as I come down.

I look between my legs. I felt a definite liquid explosion. I've touched myself before, but it's been a little bit wet. Nothing like this. His hand glistens with my moisture. "Was that okay?"

His nostrils flare. "That was fucking beautiful. I want you to come like that on my cock."

Then he pulls off his clothes. His muscles ripple with tension. In the bright light of day, I can see every line of his body, the tanned skin and dark hair. He looks like a warrior.

He pulls a small square from his wallet. A condom.

I watch, feeling suddenly shy as he rips it open and rolls it over his cock.

"Oh hell," he says, looking down at me. I'm too exposed. Even pressing my legs together does little to hide my naked body. He puts a hand between my thighs and opens me. "I'm not going to last long. Just looking at you makes me want to come."

He puts one knee on the bed and leans forward, his cock notched against my sex. "Tell me if I go too fast. Or too hard. Tell me if I'm hurting you."

"Wait," I say.

His muscles tremble with restraint. "Yeah?"

"I'm not..." God, I should have rehearsed this. That would have been weird, but this is weirder. "I'm not that kind of a virgin."

He lifts my chin until I meet his gaze. "What kind of virgin are you?"

"I'm not going to... I'm not going to bleed or anything. I don't have a hymen. It's not my first time. It's just the first time that I'm going to be—"

"Willing," he says, his teeth clenched.

"I was going to say conscious," I say, with a slightly hysterical little laugh.

"Christ," he says, pulling back, running a hand through his hair. He stalks away, clearly furious. And completely unselfconscious about the fact that he's naked and still erect.

"No, no. We don't have to stop. I don't want to stop. I just didn't want you to feel like you had to hold back or think it was strange if I didn't bleed or something."

"Let's get a few things straight, Jane Mendoza." He stalks close to me again, pulling me up to a sitting position on the bed. My legs hang over the side, not quite long enough for my feet to touch the ground. It's a tall bed. "One, it can hurt even when you're not a virgin of any kind. If you haven't had sex in a while, if you're not completely ready, if the man goes too hard… all those things can hurt you, and that's what I was concerned about."

"Oh. So maybe I didn't need to say anything."

"Two, who the fuck did that to you?"

A long sigh escapes me. I look up at the ceiling. It doesn't have any answers. "Does it matter?"

"Yes, it fucking matters."

"Is there a chance we can go back to doing what we were doing?"

"Oh, we're doing that. Don't worry. But first, you're going to give me a name."

"Why?"

"Because I'm a hypocritical bastard who demands your secrets even when I won't give you my own. Now tell me."

"It was my foster father. And maybe it was my own fault. He wasn't even home much. One night I was up late and so was he. He offered to let me try some of his beer. It didn't taste good, but he told me to finish the whole can."

"It wasn't your fucking fault. Don't say that again."

"The next morning I woke up in bed. I didn't remember anything about what happened. But there was something between my legs. I was sore and I thought… well, I think I know what he did. It was only that one time though."

"One time is too many."

"After that I mostly avoided him. And Noah was there to protect me."

Beau blows out a hard breath. "I suppose I can't hate the guy too much, then."

I don't feel sexual anymore, not after talking about my foster father, not after thinking about that night. But I don't want him to control me. I don't consider what happened that night to be sex. Beau Rochester will be my first; I won't let my foster father take that from me.

I reach out tentatively for Beau. He doesn't move as I stroke a circle across his bicep. And then a triangle. And then a square. Then I graduate to letters.

Can we start over? I ask with silent, traced letters.

He faces me. "I want to kill someone," he says, fury evident in his voice.

"Do that later."

A short laugh. "You are perfect, you know that? You're so damn strong. You're invincible. It terrifies me, how much I want you."

He presses a kiss to my forehead, my nose, my chin. The place between my breasts. My belly button. My legs fall open in surrender. And then he presses a kiss to my sex. He licks from bottom to top, lingering to draw around my clit. A circle. A triangle. A square. I let out a breathless laugh. Then he sucks on my clit in earnest, fluttering his tongue, and I moan, grasping his hair in my fists, shamelessly rubbing against his face.

Right when I'm about to come, he pulls back.

"No," I moan.

He quirks his lips. "Remember what I said. I want you squirting on my cock."

"Is that what I did?"

"That's what you're about to do." He notches his cock against my sex, and this time I don't ask him to wait. This time he presses forward, and he's right. Even without a hymen, even though I'm not a virgin in the most technical sense, it sort of hurts. It's definitely a stretching sensation. I suck in a breath, and he pushes deeper.

"Oh God, you feel good," he mutters.

With a final thrust, he pushes all the way inside. His hips are flush with my thighs.

My mouth opens on a silent cry. I feel incredibly full. Too full. I pant through the sensation.

He holds still to let me get used to him. "Okay?" he asks, his voice tense.

"Okay," I say, too high pitched to be believed.

"Tell me to stop," he says, and I hear the echo of when he said that before. In the hallway, right before he put his hand beneath my nightgown and made me come.

"Don't stop."

"Fuck," he says, and then he's pulling out and pushing back inside. Each thrust pushes deeper somehow. It feels like too much until his thumb finds my clit. He rubs using the same rhythm, and soon I'm melting against the bed, turning into a puddle of arousal.

"What number is this?" I ask, breathless.

"Number six?" he asks, more a question. "Seven?"

Another thrust inside me. "Eight. Nine. Ten." He's counting every single push, and I can't disagree. Each one feels like a revelation. Each one sends pleasure cascading through my body. Soon my hips rise up to meet him, little breathy moans escaping me each time.

He's moving faster and faster, harder and harder. I'm losing my grip on reality. Everything is a blur. Everything is sensation. He chokes on a cry and throws his head back. I watch his throat work as he comes, his tendons straining, his muscles taut. His hand holds my hips in place, leaving bruises on my skin. His other hand presses tight against my clit. The sight of him in rapture is what sends me over. I grind my hips against his sweet pressure, gasping, riding myself through the final waves of orgasm.

CHAPTER TWENTY-FIVE
JANE MENDOZA

I'M NOT COLD. I'm warm. Uncomfortably warm, actually.

I'm standing outside on the cliff where the grass and dirt are rolled back like a rug, the core of the mountain exposed. Wind whips around me, blowing my hair into my eyes. They sting.

The sky above me is filled with fog. No, it's smoke—gray and billowing.

I look down. Instead of a stormy sea, there's lava bubbling up from the center of the earth. It's red and angry and active, eating at the mountain, trying to consume it. More and more lava spurts from beneath us, making the level rise. I watch it come closer and feel the heat wash over me. Pretty soon there will be no rock left to stand on.

The lava will swallow me, and I'll become ash in its fiery waves.

A gasp. Smoke fills my throat, and I cough.

It was a dream, the lava climbing the cliffside.

I'm not standing outside; I'm in my bedroom, half-asleep. The smoke is real. It fills my nostrils, my mouth. It coats my eyes in grit.

Beau is beside me, already pushing the covers off.

"Fuck," he says, grabbing me by my wrist, dragging me out of bed.

I stumble behind him as he enters Paige's room. Then he's walking back out, carrying his niece in his arms. Thank God. *Thank God she's okay.* I run ahead down the smoke-filled stairs to make sure nothing blocks their path.

There's a fire extinguisher in the pantry, my mind supplies. It's a small thing, no match for this blaze. Assuming I could even find the fire to douse. So far the only thing I've seen is smoke. Heat seeps under my skin and behind my eyes. It radiates from the beams of the house, as if it's already on fire and I just can't see the flames.

Smoke invades my throat, and I cough— which only draws in more smoke to my lungs. It burns. Something falls in front of me—a piece of the house, about a yard of wood, still on fire. I stagger and glance behind me.

Beau has his hand on the back of Paige's head, keeping her face turned toward him.

I lead them around the obstacle and reach for

the front door. A shriek of pain escapes me, unable to be contained as the heat from the metal knob sears my palm. I use the hem of my shirt to shield myself and try again. It still burns, but I force it open for Paige's sake.

The door finally slams open, and I stumble out onto the wet grass, panting, coughing. Mr. Rochester sets Paige down a few yards away and then comes back to haul me farther from the house. I turn back, and from this angle, I can see where the fire started. Somewhere high. The attic, most likely. The flames soar to the sky even as the bottom crumbles under the weight. It feels like there's still fire in my lungs, fighting to get out. I can't stop coughing. Beau coughs too. Paige looks like she's in shock, her eyes wide, tears falling down her small cheeks.

Suddenly she lets out a scream. "Kitten!"

"Oh God." I glance back at the second floor, which is dark, the window clouded with smoke. Is the kitten still inside? I didn't see her. Then again it was so crazy, so fast, so scary. What if she was curled up in a corner, afraid, unable to meow because of the smoke?

I'm standing before I even fully form the thought, already heading back inside.

Strong arms haul me back. "Don't you fucking dare," Beau says.

I look back at him, unable to shake free. Moments pass in strange measures of time. They jump over minutes and make seconds last forever. I can feel the press of his thumb inside my elbow. I can hear his breath sawing in and out of his body, rough from the smoke. It takes only moments for me to consider—he needs to stay alive for Paige's sake. I'm the only one here without commitments, without family. I'm the only one who wouldn't be missed if I died in that house. It would be a sad thought on another day, but now it's galvanizing. This is my purpose.

"You have to let me go," I say, and it's so inadequate as an explanation, but pain flares in his eyes, as if he understands everything I'm trying to say.

He's rough as he shoves me next to Paige on the ground. "Wait with her."

"Beau," I shout, but he's already halfway there.

"Do your fucking job."

It doesn't matter if I want to argue with him more. By the time I stand up in the mud he's inside the house. It groans and quivers, the flames eating at the structural integrity.

"Come on," I say to Paige, breathless with

fear. "Let's go back."

She fights me. "We have to save Kitten."

"Uncle Beau is going to save her," I say, swallowing hard. It feels like swallowing knives. I don't know whether he will be able to or not, but there will be more than enough time for crying later if it turns out he can't. "Come on, we have to move back."

I pull her along, more rough than I would be at another time, made clumsy with urgency. Once we reach the tree line, I can breathe again. We look a mess. We're both covered in soot and mud. It streaks across our pale nightgowns. I'm shaking. Maybe because I'm afraid, but part of me also knows it's cold out. It has to be under forty degrees, and we're wearing light cotton that ends at our knees. I wish I'd thought to bring a jacket for Paige. She's going to freeze to death before we get to safety. Or my phone to call for help.

Or the kitten, while we're sending up useless prayers.

"Wait here," I say, dashing to the old shed. It's a little close to the house for safety, but I move quickly. There's a tarp inside. When I get back to her, I wrap it around her body like a blanket. Not exactly comfortable, but it should keep more body heat inside and protect her from the wind.

A faint siren reaches me on the wind, and I look down across the water to the beachfront village. Red and white lights bounce off trees. I hope that's coming for us. They can definitely see the flames from here. At least there's help on the way, but it's got to be fifteen minutes out to make it over the bridge and up the mountain.

There's a crash from inside the house, and I flinch. Beau is inside there.

Paige stands there with the army green tarp wrapped around her. She looks extra pale beneath the heavy plastic and the streaks of mud, like some kind of fairy who fell down to earth. I've seen her with a hundred different expressions— playful and angry and curious. She stares at the house with a haunted resignation. This was how she looked when she found out her parents died. I wasn't there, but I already know. This is soul-deep grief.

No. I won't let her grow up without family. I won't let Beau die, not on my watch. I'm the expendable one here. Not him.

I kneel down in front of her. "Wait here, understand? Right by this tree. Don't go any-where." I want to tell her not to go anywhere except with me or with Uncle Beau, but the truth is she may not see either of us again. Don't think like that. "Wait for the people in uniforms. They're going to come in a big fire truck with lights and sirens."

She gives me a solemn nod.

That's all I need to turn around and rush into the house. Smoke hits me like a wall. It makes me stagger back. It's so thick that the air is heavy and solid as I try to push through.

I'm disoriented. Dizzy. I barely know which way leads deeper into the house and which takes me outside again. It's like a maze without walls. I could become lost in here, never finding Beau, never finding anything. There's a shout, and I turn to the left.

The sitting room. It's where we had drinks before the dinner party. Where Beau licked me after. Now it's a disaster, the lush leather furniture covered in debris.

Beau's trapped under a massive beam that looks twelve inches wide and twelve inches deep. It spans almost the entire room. It looks almost strong enough to hold up the second floor. At least it did before it fell down. He's shouting something to me, but I can't hear.

I make my way over, tripping a few times, burning myself on hot metal.

Everything is a blur, made hazy from tears in

my eyes.

He shoves something small and warm in my hands. I'm taken back in time to when I first met him outside. The lights from his vehicle blinded me. The rain and mud made the world topsy turvy. He handed me a kitten back then and he hands me one now.

I hold her under one arm and pull with the other. It's useless. If he couldn't lift the beam himself, there's no way I can do it—and especially not one-handed.

Indecision. Uncertainty. It paralyzes me. "Go," he shouts. I can't hear him over the blaze, or maybe that's only my fear, but I can read his lips.

I've had an uneasy relationship with God since I can remember. He took my mother first. Then my father. How could someone all knowing, all seeing, allow what happened in my bedroom in my first foster home? It would be so much easier if I didn't believe in him. Then I would not have to blame him. Now I pray to a God that forsook me long ago to hold on. To let Beau live another ten seconds, twenty seconds. The thirty seconds it takes me to run the kitten outside and push her into Paige's waiting arms, her hoarse cry of relief echoing across the cliff.

Then I'm running back toward the house.

Fog and incessant drizzle have made the ground wet. My foot goes out from under me as if I'm tripping on a banana in a cartoon. I land hard on my face. That's the irony of the rain here. It's not enough to put out the fire. Only enough to make it hard to escape.

Debris blocks the entrance, but I climb my way over, wincing at splinters and burns. I'm not going to let Paige grow up without family, but if I'm honest, it's about more than her. It's about me. Somewhere along the past few months, I fell for Mr. Rochester.

It would break my heart to love him. It's already broken.

I reach the living room. His face contorts in fury when he sees me. No explanation needed. I know he's pissed at me for coming back inside the house. I couldn't wait for the firefighters. Even ten minutes could be the difference between life and death.

With both hands I pull on the edge of the beam. It barely groans in answer.

I search the room for something to use as a lever, but there are only charred remains and a lovely gold-crusted lamp that I never even noticed before which has somehow remained upright.

When I get close, Beau snatches me to his chest. He presses kisses over my forehead and cheeks. "Get the fuck out," he growls, even as he kisses me more. It's messy and elemental. We're facing our mortality together. It's more intimate than sex.

"Get out," he says again, his fist in my hair, giving a little shake to punctuate his words.

"I can't go without you," I tell him, panting against his lips.

"You'll die."

"Maybe—" I don't bother to explain with words. I only show him, pushing my legs beside his under the beam. Maybe if we can both push up at the same time, it will dislodge it.

It doesn't move. I have even less impact than I did before.

It feels like trying to lean against a wall and knock it down. Useless.

He puts his forehead against mine. "I need to let you go. You said that before. And it was right. I need to let you go, Jane. You have to go."

It's a cage. A hallway that closes at both ends. I can't leave him here to die. Not even to save myself. I stare at him as a kind of peace settles over me. There's nothing to be afraid of once you decide to die. Is this how my father felt? My mother?

Is this how Paige's parents felt?

He sees the answer written on my face.

His eyes widen. His nostrils flare. "No. No. You can't make me watch you die, Jane. You can't make me go through that." He pushes me away. "I love you."

"What?" He's never said that to me before.

"I love you, goddamn you. Get the fuck out of here."

I love you too. I want to tell him, but I don't have the breath. Or the time.

There's a shudder from the entire house. A groan.

I look up in time to see the ceiling cave in. A hand at the back of my head. It pushes me down. Strong arms shove me underneath his body. There's a loud sound.

Then the world goes black.

THE END

Thank you for reading PRIVATE PROPERTY! I hope you loved Beau Rochester and Jane Mendoza's love story as much as I do. Their story will continue in the Rochester trilogy with STRICT CONFIDENCE...

Forbidden. Commanding. Mysterious. Beau Rochester has an entire house full of secrets. And those secrets are putting Jane Mendoza in danger.

She fell in love with the one man she can't have. She should leave Maine to protect her heart, but the thread refuses to be severed. The brooding Mr. Rochester and his grieving niece are more than her job. They're her new family.

She races against time to find answers and protect the people she loves. The cliffside grows dark with the misdeeds of the past. Her heart and her sanity fight a battle, but they are both at risk.

Will Mr. Rochester learn to trust Jane? And will that trust destroy her?

SIGN UP FOR SKYE WARREN'S NEWSLET-

TER:

www.skyewarren.com/newsletter

And I'm thrilled to offer a sneak peek of THE PAWN, the USA Today bestselling full-length dark contemporary novel about revenge and seduction in the game of love…

"Wickedly brilliant, dark and addictive!"

– Jodi Ellen Malpas,
#1 New York Times bestselling author

✧   ✧   ✧

WIND WHIPS AROUND my ankles, flapping the bottom of my black trench coat. Beads of moisture form on my eyelashes. In the short walk from the cab to the stoop, my skin has slicked with humidity left by the rain.

Carved vines and ivy leaves decorate the ornate wooden door.

I have some knowledge of antique pieces, but I can't imagine the price tag on this one— especially exposed to the elements and the whims of vandals. I suppose even criminals know enough to leave the Den alone.

Officially the Den is a gentlemen's club, the old-world kind with cigars and private invitations. Unofficially it's a collection of the most powerful men in Tanglewood. Dangerous men. Criminals, even if they wear a suit while breaking the law.

A heavy brass knocker in the shape of a fierce lion warns away any visitors. I'm desperate enough to ignore that warning. My heart thuds in my chest and expands out, pulsing in my fingers, my toes. Blood rushes through my ears, drowning out the whoosh of traffic behind me.

I grasp the thick ring and knock—once, twice.

Part of me fears what will happen to me behind that door. A bigger part of me is afraid the door won't open at all. I can't see any cameras set into the concrete enclave, but they have to be watching. Will they recognize me? I'm not sure it would help if they did. Probably best that they see only a desperate girl, because that's all I am now.

The softest scrape comes from the door. Then it opens.

I'm struck by his eyes, a deep amber color—like expensive brandy and almost translucent. My breath catches in my throat, lips frozen against words like *please* and *help*. Instinctively I know they won't work; this isn't a man given to mercy. The tailored cut of his shirt, its sleeves carelessly rolled up, tells me he'll extract a price. One I can't afford to pay.

There should have been a servant, I thought.

A butler. Isn't that what fancy gentlemen's clubs have? Or maybe some kind of a security guard. Even our house had a housekeeper answer the door—at least, before. Before we fell from grace.

Before my world fell apart.

The man makes no move to speak, to invite me in or turn me away. Instead he stares at me with vague curiosity, with a trace of pity, the way one might watch an animal in the zoo. That might be how the whole world looks to these men, who have more money than God, more power than the president.

That might be how I looked at the world, before.

My throat feels tight, as if my body fights this move, even while my mind knows it's the only option. "I need to speak with Damon Scott."

Scott is the most notorious loan shark in the city. He deals with large sums of money, and nothing less will get me through this. We have been introduced, and he left polite society by the time I was old enough to attend events regularly. There were whispers, even then, about the young man with ambition. Back then he had ties to the underworld—and now he's its king.

One thick eyebrow rises. "What do you want with him?"

A sense of familiarity fills the space between us even though I know we haven't met. This man is a stranger, but he looks at me as if he wants to know me. He looks at me as if he already does. There's an intensity to his eyes when they sweep over my face, as firm and as telling as a touch.

"I need…" My heart thuds as I think about all the things I need—a rewind button. One person in the city who doesn't hate me by name alone. "I need a loan."

He gives me a slow perusal, from the nervous slide of my tongue along my lips to the high neckline of my clothes. I tried to dress profession-ally—a black cowl-necked sweater and pencil skirt. His strange amber gaze unbuttons my coat, pulls away the expensive cotton, tears off the fabric of my bra and panties. He sees right through me, and I shiver as a ripple of awareness runs over my skin.

I've met a million men in my life. Shaken hands. Smiled. I've never felt as seen through as I do right now. Never felt like someone has turned me inside out, every dark secret exposed to the harsh light. He sees my weaknesses, and from the cruel set of his mouth, he likes them.

His lids lower. "And what do you have for collateral?"

Nothing except my word. That wouldn't be worth anything if he knew my name. I swallow past the lump in my throat. "I don't know."

Nothing.

He takes a step forward, and suddenly I'm crowded against the brick wall beside the door, his large body blocking out the warm light from inside. He feels like a furnace in front of me, the heat of him in sharp contrast to the cold brick at my back. "What's your name, girl?"

The word *girl* is a slap in the face. I force myself not to flinch, but it's hard. Everything about him overwhelms me—his size, his low voice. "I'll tell Mr. Scott my name."

In the shadowed space between us, his smile spreads, white and taunting. The pleasure that lights his strange yellow eyes is almost sensual, as if I caressed him. "You'll have to get past me."

My heart thuds. He likes that I'm challenging him, and God, that's even worse. What if I've already failed? I'm free-falling, tumbling, turning over without a single hope to anchor me. Where will I go if he turns me away? What will happen to my father?

"Let me go," I whisper, but my hope fades fast.

His eyes flash with warning. "Little Avery

James, all grown up."

A small gasp resounds in the space between us. He already knows my name. That means he knows who my father is. He knows what he's done. Denials rush to my throat, pleas for understanding. The hard set of his eyes, the broad strength of his shoulders tells me I won't find any mercy here.

I square my shoulders. I'm desperate but not broken. "If you know my name, you know I have friends in high places. Connections. A history in this city. That has to be worth something. That's my collateral."

Those connections might not even take my call, but I have to try something. I don't know if it will be enough for a loan or even to get me through the door. Even so, a faint feeling of family pride rushes over my skin. Even if he turns me away, I'll hold my head high.

Golden eyes study me. Something about the way he said *little Avery James* felt familiar, but I've never seen this man. At least I don't think we've met. Something about the otherworldly glow of those eyes whispers to me, like a melody I've heard before.

On his driver's license it probably says something mundane, like brown. But that word can never encompass the way his eyes seem almost luminous, orbs of amber that hold the secrets of the universe. *Brown* can never describe the deep golden hue of them, the indelible opulence in his fierce gaze.

"Follow me," he says.

Relief courses through me, flooding numb limbs, waking me up enough that I wonder what I'm doing here. These aren't men, they're animals. They're predators, and I'm prey. Why would I willingly walk inside?

What other choice do I have?

I step over the veined marble threshold.

The man closes the door behind me, shutting out the rain and the traffic, the entire city disappeared in one soft turn of the lock. Without another word he walks down the hall, deeper into the shadows. I hurry to follow him, my chin held high, shoulders back, for all the world as if I were an invited guest. Is this how the gazelle feels when she runs over the plains, a study in grace, poised for her slaughter?

The entire world goes black behind the staircase, only breath, only bodies in the dark. Then he opens another thick wooden door, revealing a dimly lit room of cherrywood and cut crystal, of leather and smoke. Barely I see dark eyes, dark suits. Dark men.

I have the sudden urge to hide behind the man with the golden eyes. He's wide and tall, with hands that could wrap around my waist. He's a giant of a man, rough-hewn and hard as stone.

Except he's not here to protect me.

He could be the most dangerous of all.

Want to read more? Order The Pawn from Amazon, Barnes & Noble, Apple Books, or Kobo.

Books by Skye Warren

Endgame Trilogy & more books in Tanglewood

The Pawn

The Knight

The Castle

The King

The Queen

Escort

Survival of the Richest

The Evolution of Man

Mating Theory

The Bishop

North Security Trilogy & more North brothers

Overture

Concerto

Sonata

Audition

Diamond in the Rough

Silver Lining

Gold Mine

Finale

Chicago Underground series

Rough

Hard

Fierce

Wild

Dirty

Secret

Sweet

Deep

Stripped series

Tough Love

Love the Way You Lie

Better When It Hurts

Even Better

Pretty When You Cry

Caught for Christmas

Hold You Against Me

To the Ends of the Earth

For a complete listing of Skye Warren books, visit

www.skyewarren.com/books

ABOUT THE AUTHOR

Skye Warren is the New York Times bestselling author of dangerous romance such as the Endgame trilogy. Her books have been featured in Jezebel, Buzzfeed, USA Today Happily Ever After, Glamour, and Elle Magazine. She makes her home in Texas with her loving family, sweet dogs, and evil cat.

Sign up for Skye's newsletter:
www.skyewarren.com/newsletter

Like Skye Warren on Facebook:
facebook.com/skyewarren

Join Skye Warren's Dark Room reader group:
skyewarren.com/darkroom

Follow Skye Warren on Instagram:
instagram.com/skyewarrenbooks

Visit Skye's website for her current booklist:
www.skyewarren.com

COPYRIGHT

This is a work of fiction. Any resemblance to actual persons, living or dead, business establishments, events or locales is entirely coincidental. All rights reserved. Except for use in a review, the reproduction or use of this work in any part is forbidden without the express written permission of the author.

Made in the USA
Middletown, DE
29 March 2021